# *An Interview with an Underground Doctor*

## A tragedy in four parts

By C. Hensle

"The urge to save humanity is almost always a false front for the urge to rule."
H. L. Mencken

This is a work of fiction. All names, places, and events are products of the author's imagination. Any similarity to actual names, places, or events is merely coincidental.

# Part One

I guess it all began way back in 2044. I was drifting over a sea of troubles of which I was unaware, unconscious, unenlightened. To anyone else it might look like I had a good life. For five years I had worked at the same job I found when I got out of college. It was not a bad job. I thought I was good at what I was asked to do, but I did not have to try very hard.

Many of my friends did not have jobs, the economy being what it is, and had to live with their parents. I shared an apartment with three friends. On the weekends we played sports, football or baseball or basketball. For a real break we might take a trip to play golf or climb a mountain. During the week there were broadcasts of games and shows about the games we had just seen as if seeing the home run one more time would make a difference in our lives. For a particularly big game we would have friends over for pizza and beer. Occasionally, a group of us would get tickets to a game where we would drink some more beer. One or two nights a week we would end up at a bar where we would drink more beer and watch some more sports.

So, I was drifting along on a comfortable path. I had a nice job without too many demands that paid well enough for me to enjoy fun and friends. I find it hard to beat that. But it was not what I had planned. In college I had wanted to be a writer. I wrote then. I had no problem coming up with ideas to write about when I was in college. The world had seemed so important. Now, I just don't know. I seem preoccupied with the mundane in life. If those things are taken care of why bother?

I thought five years after college I would have finished my first novel and started on my second. I had no illusions about getting my first novel published especially with the state of publishing today. My first novel was always going to be my secret novel, the one that gets discovered as a lost gem. But here, five years after college, I had not written one word.

At first I blamed the job. Then I blamed my friends for being a distraction. Every day I thought I might sit down at the computer and conjure up some prose my friends needed me for this game or that. I always went. They were my friends and there was always tomorrow.

For awhile I fantasized about quitting the job and finding some quiet place to write. The thought remained a fantasy. Life was too easy. I had turned into a sleepwalker and was too scared to wake up. I had lost what made me who I was. Now I was just another interchangeable part in an insurance office or the ninth for a softball team. I still thought about being a writer, but my thoughts were about being a writer not those ideas that burned to be written down. Finally, I had to admit that I did not wake up in the morning thinking about writing and nothing else.

Okay, maybe I wasn't a writer, but that was my story and I stuck to it. One night at the bar where we usually hang out I was introduced to Joey, a friend of a friend from high school. We ended up sitting next to each other at a table and he asked what I did. I told him about the insurance office and then gave him my usual song and dance about being a writer. Then he asked the question I always dreaded, "What are you working on now?"

I told him the tale about being so busy in the insurance office I did not have much time to write and that I was looking for an idea that really excited me.

"You ought to write about OPIE," he said.

"OPIE! What the heck is that?"

"OPIE is the Office of Program Integrity and Enforcement. It is one of the most powerful and important parts of the federal government. I've been working there for six months and no one I talk to outside the agency seems to know we exist. It's so weird. I've asked people at the agency if what we do is supposed to be a secret and they tell me, 'No.' But no one knows about us."

"Okay! What do they do?"

"OPIE is responsible for the whole health system. We are the ones who make sure the system is fair and equitable. We do all the audits."

Now I could see why no one knew about OPIE. Accountants might put you in jail, but no one writes about the dashing and fearless accountant. "I don't know," I told him. "Audits don't sound very interesting to me."

"That is where you'd be wrong. OPIE audits save resources and make sure the distribution of resources is fair. But one of the most interesting things we do and the area where I work is in black market medicine. We are in charge of all enforcement in the area of black market medicine."

Black market medicine, now I was intrigued. "Tell me about black market medicine."

"It's become big business. People are getting medicines and treatments that they are not legally allowed to under the health system. It drains resources from the health system hurting everybody else. And none of these doctors or facilities is licensed putting everyone at risk.

"In a few days we are going to have a big bust. Maybe you'd like to be there? I might be able to arrange an interview with the director. She's been with agency for twenty years. She's reached legendary status."

I told him I would be interested. We exchanged information. Then the pizza and another round of beers showed up. The topic of conversation changed. I forgot about black market medicine.

About a week later I arrived at the office and found a note stuck on my computer screen. I called the number on the note. Joey answered. "Don't have much time to talk," he said. "Things are hitting the fan. If you can be there at 6:00 and you might get that story we talked about." He gave me an address on Maple. Then he hung up.

I made it through the rest of the day without really thinking about work. I wondered what I might find at 6:00.

I reached the address an hour early. It turned out to be one of those old fashioned strip malls from the last century with shops on the ground floor and offices on the second. The address was a Chinese restaurant I had been to once. They did a takeout business, but were pretty popular for sit down meals. I decided to take a look around.

I found the entrance to the second floor and, after walking up a flight of stairs, walked the length of the corridor. I didn't see anything suspicious. Next I went around to the back. There were the usual dumpsters and delivery entrances. I saw nothing unusual. Finally, I decided to tackle the restaurant. I went in, asked for the takeout menu, and looked around. I left after saying that I had some more shopping to do.

I sat in my car and watched. The restaurant appeared to do a brisk business for early on a weekday night. Other than that everything seemed so normal.

By 6:30 I began to think I might as well order some egg rolls and wonton soup. Perhaps I had the address wrong or Joey meant 6:00 a.m. not 6:00 p.m. Just when I was about to give up they showed up. Four black cars with government plates pulled up in front of the restaurant. Agents wearing jackets with 'OPIE' on the back got out and entered the restaurant. Nothing happened for awhile. Then agents appeared escorting people in white coats out of the restaurant. The people wearing white coats had their hands cuffed behind them. I got out of the car and started snapping pictures with my hand held computer. More agents came out of the building carrying computers they placed in the trunk of one of the cars.

For the next hour there were agents exiting the restaurant carrying boxes. A van arrived, loaded the white coats, and left. After an hour people started exiting the restaurant and sliding into the night. I had inched forward staying just far enough away not to get noticed, but close enough to see what was going on.

There were only two government cars left. A group of agents came out. Three of them hovered around a female. She apparently gave them some orders. They got into one car and drove away. That left one male agent and the female. The male agent appeared to be looking around. When he turned my way I recognized Joey. I waved and Joey motioned for me to join them.

Joey met me half-way and took my hand. "Justin, the Director wants to meet you." Then he said something I found very strange, "Don't be afraid."

We walked over to the Director and Justin introduced us, "Director, this is Justin Lodge that writer I was telling you about. Justin, this is Director Stricker."

"So, Mr. Lodge, what do you think about what happened here tonight?" the Director asked.

The Director stood with her back to the restaurant so her face was in shadows. All I could tell was tall, thin, short blonde hair with an edge in her voice.

"I'm not sure what happened. All I saw were some agents escorting people in white coats out of a Chinese restaurant."

"What went on here, Mr. Lodge, is that we closed down an illegal clinic that preyed on innocent people."

"In a Chinese restaurant?"

"Yes, that was clever of them. The clinic was on the second floor. These illegal clinics have learned that a large number of people entering a supposedly empty building will draw attention so they have been hiding behind a place like this one. Joseph here tells me you would be interested in writing a story. Perhaps I could answer a few questions."

"Yes, that would be helpful. Who were the people in white coats that had their hands cuffed?"

"Of course, I cannot give you names at this time, but they were the doctors and nurses that run the clinic."

"What are they going to be charged with?"

"At the very least possession of illegal drugs. All the drugs the clinic had were black market drugs which are illegal to have in your possession. Some have been manufactured by legitimate businesses, but others have been manufactured underground. The government cannot control the quality of those drugs putting people at risk. In addition we will look at tax issues, fraud, and reckless endangerment. This clinic took millions of dollars out of the system that belong to the American people. I promise you the full weight of the federal government will be used to protect the people."

"I have never heard of OPIE until Joseph mentioned it the other night. Could you tell me something about it?"

"The Office of Program Integrity and Enforcement has been around for over thirty years. We take it as a compliment that few people know of our work. The most important thing to know about the Office is our motto, 'Ensuring the health of all Americans.' We ensure fair and equal access to the highest quality healthcare available for all Americans."

With this the Director turned to Joey saying, "I think it is time we caught up with the others, Joseph. There is still a lot of work to do tonight."

Turning to me she said, "I hope you have a story to write, Mr. Lodge. I will be watching." She took my hand and almost crushed it.

I watched them drive off. There was something about the Director. I could not put my finger on it. She had a strange intensity, but what she said sounded so reasonable, important, even.

I experienced a shiver go through my body as if things were not quite right and maybe a little scary. I decided to get out of there. I got into my car, but before I started it I noticed people were still coming and going from the Chinese restaurant. Maybe I ought to look inside.

I went inside the restaurant. Ignoring the host I went down the corridor toward the restrooms. There I found an extra door with crime scene tape covering the entrance. The wood next to the lock was splintered. I pushed the door open and felt along one side for a light switch. The lights revealed a narrow stairway going up. I entered and closed the door behind me. The door had a small window that you could open and close by sliding a panel.

At the top of the stairs I found another light switch. There was a reception area with a couple of desks. The corridor was lined with chairs. I went along poking my head into the rooms on either side. Other than the signs of a search it all appeared so normal.

I put together all the photos I had taken and under a title "OPIE: Keeping Healthcare Safe" I published something on the web. The posting did not get a lot of play, but I felt a few thousand hits were appropriate for the subject. I put together a more extensive article and submitted it to several magazines. No one was interested.

I did not think I had wasted my time. I just thought it was over. I had a brief brush with OPIE and that would be it. A couple of months later Joey called. The Director wanted to see me. I was to be at OPIE's local headquarters at a specific time. No other time would do. I tried to get out of Joey the reason for the meeting, but he claimed not to know. Joey implied this was not a request.

As I disconnected I had that little shiver again. I thought over the article I had published. I did not see how the Director could object to anything I wrote. I remembered that intense edge in her voice and her promise, "I will be watching." The more I thought about it the less I wanted to keep that appointment with the Director, but the more I feared the consequences of not showing up.

The day came and I arrived at OPIE headquarters. The reception desk called up. Joey came down to escort me up. I had arrived fifteen minutes early. An hour later I was still waiting. Finally, Joey escorted me in and announced me to the Director.

When I entered the office the Director did not get up or offer a hand. She merely motioned to the one chair placed across from her. We were separated by a big desk and behind her was a wall of windows. The only light in the room was the afternoon sun streaming in, blinding me. I could not look directly at the Director.

I sat while the Director shuffled some papers in front of her. She did not appear to be in any hurry. I waited until I could not wait any longer. "Joseph did not tell me the reason I was called here. Was there something wrong with what I published on the web?"

"On the contrary we could not have written a more perfectly bland article if we had written it ourselves."

"If you are not upset about the article why did you call me here?"

"I have a job for you. One for which I will pay you a considerable sum of money. The article was just the first step. But first I want to tell you a little about the Office of Program Integrity and Enforcement. Thirty years ago when the Office started there were over 700,000 entities for which we had audit responsibility. Now partly as a result of our audits there are only about 10,000, many with revenues over a billion dollars. With so much money at stake they are fairly easy to control. Now there is a new problem, doctors working outside the system, taking advantage of people with health problems. Our job is to ensure the health of all Americans. We can't do that if we can't monitor these doctors. Essentially, these black market doctors are stealing from you, me, every one. That is where you come in, Mr. Lodge."

"I don't understand."

"We want you to arrange an interview with a black market doctor, one of the ring leaders. We have been watching him for some time hoping he would give away the rest of his network. Then he disappeared. We know he is still out there, but we cannot find him."

"I still don't get it."

"A few years ago this black market doctor gave an interview. Somehow he thinks he is saving the world. If only more people knew about the black market in medicine the world would be a better place or so he thinks. We were able to suppress the last interview. We think he would like to try again. That is where you come in. You now have a history of interest in this area. A more established writer might not want to cooperate, but you are a nobody. We have spent the last two months monitoring you. We have monitored your computer to see if anybody tried to hack it after the articles. We have researched your rather bland history and found nothing. There is nothing of interest in any of your electronic transactions though you do spend too much money on beer at that bar you and your friends frequent. We even performed video monitoring to see if you were being followed."

Suddenly the side wall lit up. "Here you are driving to work this morning. Traffic was rather heavy. Let's zoom in on this car. What is that you are doing? Are you trying to catch flies or are you singing? Makes me happy we weren't doing audio today. Here you are parking and at your desk. Here you are at lunch. Who is the young lady? She says hello and you don't manage to say anything. Here is a video of you and your friends playing basketball. You take a shot and miss, badly. I believe at one time that was called a brick. Here is some video of you and your friends at that bar. You spend a lot of time at that bar swilling beer. Faulkner and Fitzgerald drank, but at least they had some life experience. You seem to have only beer. This one is interesting. When you and your friends left the bar this fellow seemed to follow you. He turned out to be nobody. So, it appears you are entirely clean except, of course, for this video of you violating a crime scene. I forget what sort of violation that is. It is probably just a misdemeanor. I doubt you would have to spend time in jail."

The Director had set up a trap and I had walked right into it. She went on, "Let me show you one last video of you playing softball. Here you are at bat. Let's see what happens, my goodness, a big swing and a miss. I am so surprised. Sort of a metaphor for your whole boring life, don't you think?"

The side wall went dark and I was left squinting into the glare of the sun setting behind the director. "Mr. Lodge, your life is so boring that one of the more paranoid members of our security team thought you must be a plant. Having met you, I knew better.

"Mr. Lodge, I want to give you the opportunity to take a swing at something. Maybe this time you will connect. Well, do you have any questions?"

"Yes, if this black market doctor has gone so far underground that you can't find him how do you expect me to find him?"

"If you get the word out that you want to do the story he will contact you."

"And how am I supposed to get the word out?"

"The old fashioned way, bulletin boards. We know the black market network uses places like bulletin boards for communication. They know how easy it is to track down most computer communication. We have video surveillance of most of the common bulletin boards available to us. Somehow they continue to evade us."

"So, you want me to post on bulletin boards around the city that I want to do an interview with a black market doctor?"

"Yes, that is exactly what we want you to do. You won't be paid until after the interview and we need exact information on where and when the interview will be held."

"How am I going to know it's him? Won't I get some crackpots claiming to be a black market doctor?"

"He will be extremely careful. If anyone just calls you up and claims to be him don't believe him. He will watch you carefully for months before he will trust you. From now on we have to assume you are being watched. You cannot return to this building. When you leave you will leave by the rear entrance. Assume your computer and phones are being monitored. Do not speak to anyone about this. Someone may be listening. We will find someway of contacting you. If we are not in contact and you need to contact us buy a single use phone and call Joseph at this number. Just say, "Call me," and hang up. You will be contacted within 24 hours."

The Director handed me a slip of paper with a number on it. I wasn't being given a choice. I put the paper in my wallet. I saw her press a button on her desk. The door behind me opened. "Joseph will see you out now. Remember, I will be watching." I now knew exactly what she meant.

I started the next day. I made up a sign saying, "Wanted, Interview with Black Market Doctor." I put my name, address, e-mail address and phone number on the sign. I started with libraries and community centers. Every time I put up a sign I looked around to see if I could locate the security camera. After putting up the first sign I started to wave at the camera.

As I went around the city putting up signs I began to get paranoid. I would walk around a block to see if anybody was following. Sometimes I would just turn around and walk the other way. When I passed people I tried to remember their faces. Then I would turn around again and walk back looking at all the faces.

A week passed before I got my first hit. Someone called and said they were a black market doctor. They wanted to now how much I would pay for an interview. I hung up. I received more calls like that, but I was surprised at how few.

After a month I started to go around a second time. Most of my signs were still up on the bulletin boards. I was at a community center when I think I got my first hit. There was a male who was sitting in a chair in the lobby. His chair was turned so that he could see the bulletin board. It was the only chair in the lobby turned that way. He looked up from his paper when I entered. I swear he was watching when I put another sign on the board. When I left he followed me outside. I got into my car and waited. He walked past my car on the sidewalk and continued down the street turning right at the next corner. I started the car and took the next right following him. He was nowhere in sight.

I had built up an image of the black market doctor. He had to be six foot eight with fancy clothes and a fancy car. He had to have henchman the better to take advantage of the poor and the weak. Isn't that what a blackmarketeer does?

I may have been right about the henchman. A few days after I was followed out of the community center I was returning to the apartment late at night, in the garage a voice called out, "You, stop. Don't turn around." I froze. "Leave Dr. L alone!"

I heard something move behind me. I waited half expecting to be hit over the head. I waited and nothing happened. I took one step forward. When nothing happened I ran to the elevator dodging imaginary bullets.

I stopped making rounds of the bulletin boards. I had a name now or at least an initial, Dr. L. I was pretty sure he knew about me. He probably knew about me as soon as I started with the signs.

I didn't sign on for this. The Director hadn't really given me a choice. I knew she was watching everything I did. Now there was this Dr. L. I was sure he was watching. I wished I hadn't heard that name. He was easier to ignore without a name when he was just a figment of my imagination.

I had not bargained for this when I told Joey I would be interested in doing a story on OPIE. The story was supposed to be over there and my real life was supposed to be over here. They weren't supposed to bleed into each other. I would go out to play basketball with the guys. I would stop and look around. Was the guy in the car across the street watching me for Dr. L. or the Director? Maybe he was just waiting for his wife. I would remember the video and scan for the camera. If I looked hard enough I could always find one. Before long my friends started yelling at me to get in the game.

Even my personal life was shot. I had done everything on my hand held computer before. Everyone did. My whole life was on my hand held. Now every time I took it out whether to make a call or send a message I would wonder who would be monitoring what I said or typed. Would I get a friend in trouble just by being one of my contacts? I usually just put the hand held away.

Three months after I met with the Director I received a call on my phone while at work. It was a mechanical voice. The voice said that if I wanted an interview I should check into a certain hotel at 9:00 pm tonight. I was to ask for room 428, get into the room, and wait. Then he hung up.

This was the first contact that seemed legitimate. I looked around the office to see if anyone was watching. I looked at the security camera because I knew the Director would be watching. I didn't have much time to contact OPIE. I had to do it right away. Should I make the call from my desk or try the men's room? I decided to make the call from my desk. I hunkered down a little in my cubicle and called the number for Joey. When he wasn't in and I got transferred to voicemail I was so flustered I almost forgot to say, "Call me."

I did not know what to do next. Should I call Joey again? Was I going to receive a call with instructions? I had an hour until lunch. I tried to work. I was hopeless.

At lunchtime I was too anxious to eat. I walked around the block a couple of times. I walked through a couple of stores that had more than one entrance. If anybody was following me I couldn't tell.

When I got back to my desk there was an envelope with my name and 'open immediately' on it. The instructions were simple. I was to take the elevator to the third floor and enter the men's room there. I was to take the instructions with me and proceed immediately.

I slipped the instructions in my pocket and headed for the elevator. On the third floor the men's room was closed for repairs. The door opened when I tested it. I decided to enter anyway. There was a plumber working on one of the sinks. He got up, pushed past me, and locked the door. The first thing he said was, "Do you have the message we left for you?"

I pulled the envelope from my pocket. He took it, opened it, read it, and shoved it in a pocket. "What do you know?"

I told him about the call. He asked me to repeat the name and address of the hotel. He said, "Nine o'clock?" I nodded. "Tonight?" I nodded again. "Room 428?" I nodded a third time.

He took a moment before going on. "Do exactly what he told you to do. We will do the rest."

He unlocked the door and pushed me out saying, "I told you it was broken. What kind of idiot can't read a sign?"

I was worthless the rest of the day. At the end of the day I decided not to go home. The hotel was actually on the edge of town off the interstate. I drove past the hotel a few times. I stopped to get a hamburger and a shake. I couldn't finish the hamburger so I ordered another shake to go. I was in the hotel parking lot at 8:00. At 8:50 I finished off the last of my shake and got out of the car. Everything had seemed so normal. There were no big black government cars in the parking lot, no agents walking the perimeter, nothing unusual.

I entered the hotel lobby and headed for the reception desk. I had to wait while one couple checked in.

"Can I help you, sir?"

"Yes, I would like a room for tonight."

"Certainly, sir. Do you have a reservation?"

"I do. I requested room 428."

The clerk played with his computer. "That room is already occupied, sir. Perhaps you were placed in another room. If I could have your name, please?"

"Are you sure? I was supposed to meet a friend and we agreed on room 428."

"Perhaps your friend is in another room? If you would give me a name I could check."

"That's not really a problem. I'll just go up. I'm sure my friend is in room 428."

"I'm afraid that would not be a good idea, sir. We try to protect the privacy of our clients, but you could use the house phone to call the room."

I smiled and thanked him for his help. Across the small lobby there was a phone. I dialed 428. A woman answered. "Hello, my name is Justin Lodge and I'm looking for Dr. L."

"There is no one here by that name. You must have the wrong room number," she said and hung up.

I slowly dropped the phone on its receiver. I was confused. Was this just a mistake or was I being manipulated? And by which side? Perhaps this was a trial run to see whether I would follow directions. I went back to the desk.

"Any luck, sir?"

"No, you were right. Perhaps you have another room reserved for me. My name is Justin Lodge."

The clerk started entering my name. "I'm sorry, sir, I've checked under 'Lodge' and under 'Justin.' We have no reservation under those names."

"Do you have any rooms available for tonight?"

"No, sir, we are full. It is July 3rd. Are you sure you have the correct hotel?"

I didn't want to go there as I had no idea what other hotel it could be. I had one other card to play. I stared directly in the eyes of the clerk. I did not want to miss any reaction if it was there. "Perhaps the reservation is in my friend's name. He is a bit of an eccentric. He goes by the name 'Dr. L.'"

The clerk hesitated just a second. He made a show of checking the computer. "I'm sorry, sir. The computer shows nothing under 'Doctor' and nothing that would fit under 'L.' If you are looking for a room for the night we have a sister hotel at the next exit, I could call to check on availability?"

"Yes, I would appreciate that."

The clerk made the call and I tried to listen. When the clerk made the connection he switched to Spanish and the only thing I could make out was my name. When he hung up the phone he returned his attention to me. "I have made you a reservation at our sister hotel, sir." He used a map to give me detailed instructions to get to the other hotel. When he finished he thanked me and wished me a good night. I thanked him. It was all so normal.

I was deep in thought trying to figure out what to do next. As I exited the hotel a father and teenage daughter were entering. He held the door for his daughter, swung around, and his suitcase banged me on the knee. I went down in pain. The father and daughter were very apologetic and helped me to my feet. I limped away to my car.

In my car I had a decision to make. Do I try to contact OPIE or just go? I knew someone would be watching. If they saw me making a call I might blow the whole thing. I reached into my pocket for my hand held and found nothing. After cursing I had a thought. The father and daughter were a pickpocket team. I looked back at the hotel entrance. I couldn't do anything about it now and, maybe, it was better. I was going to that other hotel.

I pulled the car out of the parking place and headed for the exit. In the rear view screen I saw another car pull out and start after me. Suddenly an old gas powered clunker pulled out of a parking space in front of the other car and seemed to die. I hesitated at the exit, but a car had pulled behind me and was honking his horn. Ignoring what was happening behind me I headed for the other hotel. I was in the middle of it now. I didn't know whether I was taking a swing at something or someone was taking a swing at me. Despite the knots in my stomach I had to see it through to the end.

I followed the clerk's directions to the other hotel, checked in, and waited.

# Part Two

They gave me room 222. It was a standard hotel room with a king size bed. There was a table with a couple of chairs. A sliding door led to a balcony. I couldn't lock the door from the inside, though. There wasn't one of those latch things you swing over to lock it.

I sat down at the table and played with my micro-recorders. These things were so cool. I had bought two so I had a back up. They were only the size of my thumb, but could record up to 24 hours. I kept setting and resetting the sound levels. I wanted to make sure I didn't end the interview and find I hadn't set one of the recorders right.

I was so busy playing with my toys I almost missed him. I heard a scratch and looked up. At first all I could see was a big, old time slouch hat and trench coat. The hat came off and he held a finger to his lips to keep me quiet. He walked around the room checking here and there. After tossing his hat and coat on the bed he sat down at the table.

He was not what I expected. He could not have been more than five foot six with white hair and a smile. I think it is the smile I will always remember. He wore an old tweed jacket and a bow tie. We sat there for a minute just taking each other in when suddenly he reached into his pockets and dropped a couple of objects on the table. "Thought you might want this," he said.

It was my hand held computer and its battery. "Sorry about the knee. I hope Freddie didn't hurt you too bad, but we couldn't take a chance on you being tracked by it. That's why you weren't asked for payment at the desk. Any electronic transaction would pop up on their monitors. You'll also find that parts of your car have been disconnected. There are so many ways to track these electronic vehicles that they didn't bother to plant a homing device. Then there was the video feed from the hotel security cameras. We couldn't take a chance someone was checking video feeds looking for you."

"You've been very careful. How many people do you have working for you?"

"I don't think you understand. I just have a lot of friends. They take good care of me."

"Okay. How do you want to do this? I've got these two recorders to make sure I don't miss anything. You don't mind?"

"No, not at all."

After performing a couple of sound checks I began, "The following is an interview with a black market doctor."

He interrupted me, 'I prefer the term 'underground doctor.' It does not sound so sinister and, I think, is more accurate."

"Very well! The following is an interview with an underground doctor. The date is July 3rd, 2044 and the time is 11:35. Please state your full name and date of birth for the record."

"No."

"We've both spent a lot of time and energy making this interview happen. The more details I have the better the story it will make."

"There are others I need to protect at least from harassment if not prosecution. For the purposes of this interview you can refer to me as Dr. L. If that is not good enough we can end the interview right now. "

"Sit down. Sit down, old man. I understand completely. I'm just trying to write the best story I can. Certainly, you can understand that. Now where would you like to begin?"

"With my father, he was a doctor, a family practitioner. I was lucky to practice with him for over ten years before he retired. I always thought he was a great man even though some would say he was only a family practitioner. I think it was mainly that he loved his patients and they loved him. I found that very attractive as a way of life and I wanted it for myself.

"It was the year they passed the healthcare bill. My father worried about how we were going to keep the patient as the number one concern in medicine, that when the federal government took over instead of making decisions on a medical or management basis we would make health care decisions based on politics or budgetary or interest group concerns. The patient had finally reached the top rung in medical concerns. Now the patient would come sixth. He always said that even if we had a perfect healthcare system it would only last until the next session of Congress. Then he told me about a member of Congress who said, "We should control everything." As my father saw it the only way to control everything is to police everything."

I interrupted, "So, what you're saying is that your actions as an underground doctor are about your hatred of the police."

"Now, if you continue to interrupt me we will never finish. And I do not hate the police. My father and I always had a lot of officers in our practice. I always thought the police in our country, with a few exceptions, have gotten it right, but compare the motivation of 'To Serve and Protect' with that of 'controlling' and you end up with a different type of policing.

Add to that the powers of life and death, forcing doctors to consider the value to society over the life of the individual, and then have the state define the values of society instead of society defining the values of the state, well, we fought most of the twentieth century against states that believed that way. You might even say that we've been fighting against that since July 4th, 1776. Then there's the problem of enforcement by a faceless bureaucracy just following the rules and regulations, just following orders. Some of the worst crimes of the twentieth century were just following orders."

"So, you fear the power of bureaucracy?"

"You don't listen very well. Everything isn't about fear and hate."

"Okay. How about money? Is there a lot of money in this underground business? Can you really make a living this way?"

"It is interesting that you should put it that way. For me it is about living. It is my life. You still aren't listening, though. First you accuse me of fear and hate. Now you accuse me of greed. The biggest fee I ever collected was a pecan pie. You know, you remind me of an administrator I once knew. He told me that only four things motivate people, greed, fear, hate, and love. You've accused me of hate and fear. Now you accuse me of greed. The only one of those four that has real power is love. The state doesn't understand love. The state can't use love. Therefore, the state fears love."

"Perhaps we should skip the philosophy and get on with your story."

"I just thought you might appreciate some of the background. As I said I practiced for over ten years with my father. Less than two years after healthcare reform passed my father retired. He told me he wished me luck, but as doctors had always been trained in the ultimate humanist value of the individual human life he did not see how it was going to work.

"I held on for about five years. The regulations and mandates of the federal government were driving up the costs of solo practice. The first real problem I noted was being locked out of prescribing certain medications by the mandated computer prescription software. It was a rarity so I did not give it much thought. It was worse for doctors who practiced in hospitals. Most everything they did was rigidly controlled. For family docs like me, we just found our choices becoming more and more restricted with time. The rules were coming out of a central committee. Or did they call it a policy bureau?

"Then one day we found that someone had hacked our government mandated computer system. I thought I needed to report it to the authorities as some sort of privacy violation, but I wanted to find out as much as I could first. I hired a cyber investigator and after a couple of thousand dollars he told me it was the Feds who had breached the system and it was perfectly legal. After that I got audited two years in a row. Why you had to audit someone whose computer you could enter legally I'll never know. It was more of a hassle than anything else. I talked to some of my friends in solo practice. They had been audited. We came to the conclusion that they were targeting solo practices. The last step was when they passed a law making the doctor responsible for the cost of the audit. Those of us who could retire, retired. The rest of us sold out to put a layer of management between us and the feds.

"It took only two years before the practice I joined sold out to a larger clinic employing thousands of doctors at different locations. I was assigned to the main clinic. The first time I walked into the new clinic building I thought about Orwell's '1984.' In that everything was dingy, falling apart. The new clinic was bright and shiny with a two story atrium. I thought about the old office I occupied with my father for all those years. It could not compare. I remember thinking that perhaps the future was not that bad after all.

"The new clinic was all about volume and the computer. With the decrease in reimbursement we were expected to see more patients and spend less time with patients. It was counter to everything I valued in medicine, but it was not as bad as the computer. With the small amount of time we had with each patient all the information was put into the computer by ancillary staff. The computer spit out a diagnosis and a treatment plan. I still tried to spend some time with each patient and the treatment plans I always considered them to be just suggestions.

"I was there about six months when I was scheduled for an appointment with the Chief of Family Practice in his office. Now the Chief hadn't seen a patient in years, but he always walked around in his white coat greeting everyone by their first name. I had no idea what to expect when I walked into his office. He was sitting at his desk, got up, extended a hand, and indicated a chair for me to sit.

"'I always like to have the new employees in for a chat after six months,' he said. He turned to his computer. 'I see your wait times are well beyond what we find acceptable, but despite that your patient satisfaction scores are as high as anyone in the clinic. I guess when patients finally get to see you they enjoy the experience. Ah, I see here is the problem. Your production is low. When we start new doctors we always book them lightly at first until they can get used to the computer. Usually by six months their production has picked up. Let's talk about that a bit.'

"I mumbled something and the Chief went on, 'The clinic works off a global budget that requires us to give care to a high volume of patients. That is where the computer comes in. We have spent millions and millions to develop expert software to handle all the routine problems. These options have been created by data mining millions of patients and can consider hundreds of data points per patient. Certainly, you don't think you know better than the computer?'

"I've found there is no point arguing with a true believer so I kept quiet. 'Good,' he said. He went on, 'All your co-workers we have trained to be experts at what they do. None of them have the overarching knowledge that you have, but in their area they are experts. You can trust what they have put in the computer 100%. Now here is where you come in. You are the most expensive professional in the world to produce and we have to make the most of that talent and knowledge. What we want you to do is verify and validate. Verify and validate. You are the only one who can put it all together. You should look at the results on the computer and determine if the treatment plan makes sense. The computer will give you a complete plan based on everything in the computer so nothing will be overlooked. And when you accept the plan the rest of the clinic goes into action. We have experts on smoking cessation, on weight loss, on diabetic care, and other areas that will follow up with the patient. These are all areas you could never be an expert in. Now you don't have to be. We have disease management programs to follow patients at home and keep them out of the clinic or hospital. That is something you could never have time for.'

"The Chief had been looking at his computer screen throughout. Now he stopped and looked at me. 'There is, of course, another problem,' he said. I had no idea what he was talking about so I just sat there. 'Your co-workers are all worried about their bonuses.' Again, he stopped and waited. I still had no idea what he was talking about. 'Your co-workers are all paid a bonus based on the productivity of your group. In addition we pay bonuses for meeting certain numerical standards such as the number of smokers referred to our smoking cessation team, the number of pounds lost in targeted individuals, and the number of patients referred for certain cancer screening tests. Now, I don't want you to worry about this now. We've stepped in and guaranteed the bonuses this year, but if your production doesn't pick up we may have problems finding anyone that will work with you.'

"I was so stunned I did not know what to say. 'There is, unfortunately, still another problem. We have had specific complaints that your co-workers find working with you demeaning. You have to remember that your co-workers are all trained professionals. We have trained them to be experts in their specific areas. They all take pride in what they do. When you go back and check everything they do they feel it expresses a lack of trust. I have personally reassured them that what you are doing is just an expression of your training. That once you were used to working with professionals of their caliber you would have no problem trusting them.'

"He stopped and waited a few seconds before going on, 'This last problem is actually the most serious. We have spent a lot of time building a culture of teamwork. Someone who doesn't respect his co-workers doesn't fit into our culture. That culture makes it possible for us to do a lot more for our patients.'

"With this last the Chief stood up and extended his hand. I was being dismissed. 'I want to thank you for coming in today,' he said, 'I think this conversation was a step in the right direction. I want you to know that it is very important to all of us that you are happy here.'

"I turned and started to leave. As I reached the door I turned to ask him, 'Would it be possible to rearrange my exam rooms? I think I can be more efficient if I can work on the computer and face the patient at the same time.'

"The Chief pointed his finger at me. 'There,' he said, 'that is the type of thinking we're after. Just show us what you want and we'll make it happen.'

"As soon as I left his office I went into the men's room, found an empty stall, and sat down. I broke out in a sweat. This was so far from what I valued in medicine. I didn't know what I was going to do. I was already seeing more patients a day than at anytime in private practice and now they wanted me to see more. It was industrial medicine, high volume piecework on an assembly line. I was just a 'co-worker' whose every motion was measured so it could be managed. My co-workers informed on me. And the threat was there, wasn't it. Conform or you will be gone. The costs of setting up a private practice had gone through the roof. The city and the surrounding area were dominated by three big clinics. They claimed to be competitors, but all the docs thought it was an unholy alliance. Even if I decide to try another clinic could I really expect anything to be different?

"I did not see where I had any choice. I still had children to put through school. I decided I would play their game. I was too scared not to. I would become an industrial doctor and break all records. I did and I hated every minute of it.

"So, out of fear I compromised. I became a star. I found every way to save time. I cut every corner. The Chief of Family Medicine was taking full credit for my turn around. He even assigned me young doctors to mentor. I thought I had seen it all when I spent a morning with a young doctor and all she did was walk in the room, introduce herself, and look at what the computer said. A whole morning and she never touched a patient. I thought of telling someone, but I didn't think anyone would understand.

"Then there was Jeff. Almost his whole practice was electronic. If you were willing to buy the home monitoring devices that hooked into the computer Jeff and his co-workers would monitor you at home. He would spend 80% of his time on his hand held computer answering the questions his staff couldn't. Sometimes he would see patients by video conference. Jeff told me one time that physical contact was overrated. I wonder how his wife felt about that. Still, he had to see patients a few hours a week. When Jeff did show up at the clinic he was just so depressed at the prospect of actual face to face contact I had to wonder how he ended up in Family Medicine. Jeff was always trying to find someone to see his patients for him. One time he even offered to pay me to do it for him.

"A couple of years later something happened that saved me and was probably the start of my underground career. The clinic had a cafeteria, but I tried to get out of the building for lunch a couple of times a week. One day I was approached by a man in his thirties. Let's call him John. John introduced himself and asked if I remembered his parents.

They had been long time patients of first my father and then myself. It took a little prodding, but I did remember them, Cliff and Gerry, wonderful people. That was when John asked if he could see me as a patient. I assured him that would be no problem. Just make an appointment with the clinic. I still saw new patients every day. But that was not what he meant. John wanted to see me privately. Something clicked inside my head. Did he have something sinister to hide? What would happen if the clinic found out? I thought about it for a minute. I told him, no, it made no sense. I could do a lot more for him at the clinic.

"John nodded and I thought that was the end of it. Instead he un-slung his backpack, took out a box. He gave it to me and asked me to open it. There were military medals in the box. I recognized a couple of silver stars and a couple of purple hearts. I asked John where he had gotten all the medals. Afghanistan, mostly, he answered.

"Then John made a little speech. 'Doc,' he said, 'I went into the military because I believe in freedom, not just for the people of the United States, but for the people living in the lands where I fought. To me freedom means taking your life in both hands and never letting go. There is no freedom without choice. I am making my choice not to have my medical records in their damned computer. I want your help, Doc, and I'm willing to pay for it.'

"That last bit I didn't really care about. I sat there staring at all those medals. John was a real, live hero who had put his life on the line. 'You know I can't write any prescriptions or order any test without them ending up in the computer and the authorities finding out?' I told him.

"'Don't you worry,' John said, 'that will be my problem. You just tell me what I need. I'll do the rest without involving you.'

"The problem was the unknown is a little scary. There were rumors of what happened to doctors trying to work outside the system. Everything had to be in the computer so it could be 'managed.' I looked into John's eyes and then back at the box with all the medals. How could I not help him? I made a decision. 'Be at my house at 7:00 tomorrow night,' I told him and gave him the address.

"The next night John showed up a couple of minutes before 7:00. It was great. I examined him. We talked. It was like being a doctor again. I had some folders from my old office. At the end of the visit I wrote everything up and I gave him the folder. I was worried what might happen if a medical record was found in my home. I told him I could not charge him, but he paid anyway. I took his money and put it in a box in the bottom drawer of my desk.

"A couple of weeks later he came back. Somehow he had gotten the medication I recommended and the lab work he needed. I did not ask how he did it. I didn't want to know.

"Over time other patients found me. I always handled it the same way. I gave them the chart so I wouldn't have evidence around. I never charged the patients and they always paid. I discovered this about the patients I saw outside the clinic. They all felt the system took away their choices. They understood choice, particularly the ability to make choices about their own bodies, as being integral to their understanding of liberty.

"It was a wonderful experience being able to spend time with patients, getting to know them. It was what I went into medicine to do. This went on for years and it was really what kept me going through the grind of the clinic.

"Eventually, it fell apart. I never knew what to do with the money. In the end I decided to deposit the money in the bank and declare it as income on my tax return. I was too scared not to declare the income. I gave most of it to charity, but there it was on my tax return. It was after my wife developed an unusual form of leukemia. Conventional therapy had given her a brief remission. Vaccination had not worked. The next step was a stem cell transplant. That was when the Director walked into my office. She had worked at the clinic for awhile after residency. Then she decided to work for OPIE. Her climb had been rapid and she had just been promoted to the local director's position. After the usual greetings she started right in. 'My office is in the habit of using data mining to monitor any suspected individual,' she said. I had no idea why I should be a 'suspected individual' so I kept my mouth shut. 'Imagine my surprise when your name turned up as having an undocumented source of income,' she said. I waited. 'Video surveillance has shown a pattern of individuals visiting your house in the evening,' she said. It was her turn to wait, but I had nothing to say. Finally, she went on, 'We can't have this behavior. All the information needs to be in the computer so we can manage the health of the nation.' And there was the veiled threat. 'If this continues I don't know what will happen.'

"We sat there looking at each other. The Director is a beautiful woman. I stared into those unnaturally blue eyes of hers and saw something scary. She was absolutely certain she was right and you were wrong. For people like that anyone who disagrees with them is illegitimate and deserves to be crushed. I thought of my wife. Would she, could she prevent my wife from getting her transplant? I didn't know and didn't want to find out. At last I just said, 'I understand.' The Director told me how happy she was we could come to an agreement and avoid any messy enforcement problems. That was the end of the first phase of my underground career.

"Two years later my wife was dead. Of course her death was an unpleasant experience, but it was made worse by the medical care she received. Her doctors had tried what they could try. They were ready to move on. In a very real sense they abandoned her.

"Things started to go wrong for me at the clinic. I had a patient who refused a colonoscopy for cancer screening. His stool had always turned up negative for cancer cells so I never thought anything about it. I went through the process of informing him of the need for a colonoscopy and when he refused I clicked the appropriate box and informed him of alternatives which he always refused. One day he shows up in the ER with a bowel obstruction. It was cancer. When he gets out of the hospital he comes to see me. He tells me that because he refused a colonoscopy the clinic was refusing to cover his cancer treatments. Isn't there anything I could do? I looked him in the eyes. I know he can't afford any treatments. I tell him I'll see what I can do.

"I knew this is going to stink, but I've known this patient from when I practiced with my father. He had followed me to the clinic. I couldn't abandon him now. I arranged to see the chief medical officer of the clinic. I told him I had made a mistake in assuming my patient wouldn't want a colonoscopy and the last few years I had just checked the box without asking. Now the CMO was my age and probably thought I was stretching the truth. He called in the nursing director and asked me to tell my story again. When I did the stuff really hit the fan. There was no longer any question of my patient getting treatment, but I was a different story. I would have to be re-educated. They proceeded to discuss me as if I wasn't even in the room. I sat there wondering if the head nurse knew the type of people who used the term 're-educate' in the twentieth century.

"Then there was the smoker problem. One year the clinic wanted to motivate us to crack down on smokers. The powers that be decided that any group that had less than 2% active smokers would get a bonus. This led all the other family practitioners in the clinic to dump all their smokers. I was the only doctor not dumping smokers so they all ended up on my panel. Needless to say my group did not qualify for a bonus and I had a mutiny on my hands, but I couldn't turn patients away just to make a bonus. They needed my care.

"The issues with the smokers and the colonoscopy were just symptoms of a bigger but more subtle problem. When government pays for your health care the government has an interest in your behavior. Obese people who do not lose weight are treated with contempt instead of compassion. Diabetics who have poor control of their blood sugar because they don't adhere to a diet or don't exercise are thieves. I saw this in the way my co-workers treated patients, the way they talked among themselves. Sometimes doctors can be the worst ones. In their zeal to cure everyone they want to control everything. So, we go from a history where we are told that we have unalienable rights given us by our Maker to a society where our rights are delineated by government without the consent, without the knowledge of the governed. Odd that one of the major drivers of this change is the cost of heath care.

"I see that I am losing you. This philosophic discussion of unalienable rights is not something you can relate to, but men and women have died for these ideas. Today, this is your society. You don't really know anything different, can't relate to the past. I'll cut the philosophy short, but I tell you this. The day will come when you understand what I am talking about. Now, I'll get back to my story.

"As time went by I became more and more irritated with the computer. The choices presented always seemed to accent one thing, saving money. I started adding my own choices to what the computer gave me. I got away with it for awhile. Then I was called in and given a talking to. Didn't I know that the clinic was paid by how closely it followed computer protocols? Didn't I know I was costing everyone in the clinic money? I said I would try to do better, but I was just getting fed up.

"The clinic was becoming an obnoxious place to work. I would go to a medical meeting and talk to my old friends working in other parts of the country. They would have rallies of all the employees to get them all charged up. Everyone was supposed to love everyone else. And, of course, it was enforced by everyone informing on everybody else. The key here was that it was my old friends who noticed this. For the younger doctors it was just business as usual.

"George was my oldest friend in the clinic. He was a few years older than I was and remembered my father well. We would have lunch together at least once a week. One day at lunch he tells me that one of the bureaucrats that over sees the clinic was in his office and requested what was then a new 3-D scan. He was so happy when he could show the bureaucrat that the computer wouldn't allow it. The next day he gets an e-mail saying the test had been ordered by the clinic chief anyway. Then George told me some more bad news. One of our oldest family practitioners had just retired. George claimed that this other doctor was forced out after the clinic found out he was seeing some patients on the side. A chill went up my spine.

"Years before I had a patient with a recurrent sinusitis. She had cleared twice before with a course of antibiotics, but now she was back for the third time. I wanted to get a scan of her sinuses, but the computer wouldn't let me. One of the options was for referral to an Ear, Nose, and Throat doc so I decided to go that route. Eighteen months later she was dead. They had found a tumor that was so far advanced that the only thing that could be done was palliative radiation. When I ran into the ENT doc I told him how relieved I was that I had referred the patient to him for a scan. He told me the computer wouldn't let him get a scan either.

"I discussed this with George who told me that my problem was that I didn't know how to lie. All I had to was put into the computer the information that would kick out the results I wanted. He told me to be careful. If I did that too often I would be caught.

"I never did change the info in the computer. I was always too scared. I had another patient with a sinusitis. It just did not smell right to me. I thought back to that patient who had died, who I might have been able to save if I had a little more guts. So for the first time I changed some of the entries so the computer would allow me to order a scan. I ordered the scan and, sure enough, she had a tumor. I had saved her life.

"A few weeks later I was called into the office of the head of the clinic. With him were the Chief of Family Medicine and the Chief Medical officer of the regional network. These were the big doctors, the ambitious ones in the new order of medicine. I always considered myself one of the little doctors just trying his hardest to take care of the patient sitting in front of me. I guess I should have taken pride in the collection of talent required to fire me. I knew that was what they were there for the second I stepped into the room. They knew I had changed the entries. Getting a scan on a first time sinusitis was so unusual that the computer flagged the visit for audit. It didn't matter that I had been right and saved the patient's life. There was a time when being right would have mattered.

"For a second I thought of fighting, but I was ready to go. The practice of medicine had changed so much since I started and I had made so many compromises. I went home at night exhausted. I was being burned out by the pace of work. Mostly I was burned out by not living my values. I was not cut out to be a cog in some corporate machine. Nor could I treat my patients as anything but individuals. So, despite being an otherwise model doctor who was loved by patients and enjoyed good relations with nurses I had lost my career to a computer. I took the offered buy-out, worked my ninety days, and left.

"I sat around the house for awhile. I visited family, my daughter on the right coast, my son on the left. I probably should have moved to be near one of them, but I like it here in the middle. This is my hometown.

"As time went by I became more and more depressed. I had lost the two most important things in my life, my wife and my career. I finally reached a point where I did not care whether I lived or died. I believe my Hindu friends call it 'moksa', liberation.

"I sold my house. I gave my children and grandchildren all the money I could without tax problems and put the rest in a trust. I moved into a one room apartment near the office I had shared with my father. If I didn't care whether I lived or died there was no need for health insurance so I didn't bother signing up for any. I even took it one step further. I took a hammer to my dog tag. That's right. That stupid microchip personal health record we all have to carry with us at all times, I gave it six or seven blows with a hammer. I haven't worn one since.

"I spent my time meditating, listening to classical music, and walking around the old neighborhood. Sometimes I would run into old patients or their families. The questions were always the same. Was I still practicing? Was there anyway I could be their doctor? I always told them I was retired, didn't even have a license. They were nice enough to say I was too young.

"Slowly I developed a delight in the world. I can't say I had more joy than when we were a family with the kids growing up. It was different. I had always been a worrier. I worried about my children. I worried about my patients. I worried about retirement in a future that I may not see. Now I lived from second to second. When I went for a walk I felt the warmth of the sun on my back, at night the cool breeze against my cheek. I heard the laughter of children and the voice of my fellow man. The sounds of the city became a symphony of endless variety. The sounds of nature were the voice of God. Being caught in the rain was no longer a nuisance, but the experience of a miracle.

"I became a connoisseur of sunsets. I often spent an afternoon walking to some vantage point to watch the sun go down and the evening walking home. I had seen a spectacular sunset one evening at that hillside park across town. It was so beautiful that I stood up and applauded the glory of the evening. There were a few other people in the park watching the sunset. They stood up and applauded with me. Pretty soon we had quite a cheering section for the Maker of the sunset.

"It was on the way home that something happened to change my life. It had gotten late, but I never bothered about the time. I was enjoying the feeling of walking, placing one foot in front of the other, when a voice said, 'Give me your money!'

"I looked up to see a young man with a gun. He held it close to his body, out of the light. I thought for a second. I had to check my pockets. I often went out without money, but sometimes, when I know

I'm going to be out late, I will bring along a five dollar bill. I didn't find anything so I said, 'I don't have any money with me, but if you'd like to come to my apartment I might have some money there.'

"He asked how far that was. I told him three or four miles. Then he asked if I had a watch or anything else that might be valuable. I didn't have anything. 'Man, you're poorer than me,' he said. 'What did you do that you're so poor now?'

"I told him that I had been a doctor. Then he asked, 'What did you do, kill someone?'

"I thought for a second. 'No,' I told him, 'I saved someone's life.'

"He put the gun away saying, 'I've got to hear this.' We walked over and sat on some steps. We talked for hours. His name was Rodney and he was quite the natural philosopher. When I finally got up to head home he insisted on walking me home. He didn't want anything to happen to me.

"A month later I was walking home through the same neighborhood when Rodney pops up. He had been looking for me. Rodney had told his mother about the doctor who had been kicked out for saving someone's life and she wanted to meet him.

"Rodney's mom was a wonderful lady with a great sense of humor. She loved her son, but she had to needle him just a little. It was late at night, but, no matter, she was going to cook something. I rarely ate and wasn't really hungry, but it would have been impolite to refuse. We sat there chatting while she cooked and I learned all about Rodney's two sisters and the grandchildren. She turned out to be a good cook. I thought it was unfortunate because I hadn't food that tasty in years. It brought back a lot of memories.

"On the way home Rodney told me his mother had cancer. He didn't trust the doctors so he didn't believe his mother was getting good treatment. I assured him she was getting good treatment. It was just high volume and efficient, but I had been there and understood his doubts.

"I asked questions as we walked and thought I recognized delays in diagnosis and treatment. It was the usual story in a system where no one takes ultimate responsibility. Then there was the issue of her age. In a system that questioned the value of aggressive treatment in someone her age I could imagine her slipping down the priority slide.

"A couple of months passed. I saw Rodney a couple of times. I always asked about his mom. She was not doing well. From what he told me I knew she didn't have long.

"One night Rodney showed up at my door. He just said, 'Doc.' He didn't have to say more. The look on his face told me everything. I told him to wait, I would get my coat. I got my coat from the closet and the edge of my vision caught my old doctor's bag in the back of the closet. I couldn't throw it out and now I saw it without intending to do so. I wiped the dust off the bag, joined Rodney at the door, and said, 'Let's go.'

"When I arrived at her apartment it was easy to see that Rodney's mom did not have long. I went through the motions of an exam and asked a lot of questions which just confirmed my initial impression. Mostly I was just there sitting at the bedside which seemed to calm both Rodney and his mom. I understood what happened. The system had tried. Now that she was failing the calculus was bad. She was older. There was a limit to the resources the system would spend on a failure. So they moved on. The problem was those left behind felt abandoned. I knew that feeling all too well.

"I sat with her for several hours. She was unfailingly gracious. Her sense of humor lasted, too. I think she felt you might as well laugh until the end. I thought a hospice nurse would show up the next day, but I went back to visit several times. She was dead within a week.

"I went to the funeral, met his sisters and his nieces and nephews. I cried. I thought I was beyond that. The last few years it had been just me and the world. I hadn't let anything personal in. Oh, there were people I said hello to on a regular basis, I even knew some of their names, but I didn't know them

"I had been living a life beyond fears, beyond desires. I tried to return to that life, but Rodney would not let me. Over the next few months he visited me a couple of times a week. Each time he insisted I needed to return to being a doctor, that there were others who needed my help. Finally, I got angry with him, told him he just didn't understand. Anger, another emotion I thought I had put behind me.

"Then the weirdest thing happened. People just showed up at my door. I told them all no, but they all begged for my help. I would look at their faces, see the pain and desperation, and always relented. Some felt abandoned by the system. Some no longer trusted the system. Others just could not get what they needed from the system. Then there was the strangest group, the ones who had been ejected from the system. I had heard about this when I was still working. No one was ever sure whether this was just a computer glitch or some form of punishment for a sin real or imagined.

"So, I went with them. I would ask a lot of questions and go through an exam. There was not much I could do. I could not order test or medications. Basically, I offered advice and kindness. The system is very good at supplying the technical component of healthcare, but kindness is a different problem. There is a difference between customer service and compassion.

"Occasionally there would be someone with an acute problem. I would have to tell them that no matter how much they distrusted the system it was their only hope. I would tell them what to say, what to expect, and what to ask for. Sometimes I would just invite the person into my apartment and we'd talk about their problem. All of them said the same thing, they had no choice and I would remember my first underground patient who had been decorated so many times for bravery telling me that freedom means having choices.

"The amazing thing was that none of these people expected a free ride. They all offered to pay, even the poorest ones. I always refused to take their money telling them that maybe they'll be able to help me someday.

"After months of this I made the decision to embrace it. I made the decision to return to the sorrows of this world. I've never been happier."

He stopped talking. I had gotten so used to the rhythm of his speech that it took me awhile to realize that he wasn't going on. It took me even longer to see the tears.

"Are you okay?" I asked him. "Would you like a drink of water or something?"

"No, I'm fine. It's just that I owe those people who trusted me so much. When I was forced into retirement at the clinic they treated me like a thief. They claimed I was stealing from society all over a sinus scan that saved a patient's life. The truth was what I had done was subversive. My independent action questioned what they believed in so they had to turn me into something evil and make me feel worthless. The irony is that I ended up being redeemed by a thief.

"I started making rounds on a daily basis. I would go out with my doctor's bag in broad daylight, a throwback to an ancient tradition. Usually I would see only one or two patients, rarely as many as four. Most of them were ill as opposed to management of some stable chronic condition. I wasn't able to do much for them. Most of them just needed advice which sometimes was that the system was their only hope. Others just needed someone to listen to them. It was a lot of fun and as I was not charging any fee or prescribing any medications I did not think I was breaking any laws. I even told every patient that I no longer had a license.

"I started to hang out at the library so I could use the computers to keep current. One day someone bumped into me. When I had finished putting my books back in place I found a note saying that I should be in the men's room in ten minutes. When I got to the men's room there was a sign saying that it was closed for repair. I decided to try anyway. The door was unlocked. I stepped inside. A hand pulled me into the room. I had just a few seconds before the lights went out. I heard the lock on the door click into position. A voice said, "Just stand right there until your eyes get used to the dark."

"In a couple of minutes I was able to make out shapes. Then the stranger switched on a flash that hung from his belt and aimed at the floor. There was just enough light to get around without falling. The stranger turned on some music.

"Finally, I asked him, 'What the heck are you doing?'

"He introduced himself as an underground doctor. When I didn't say anything he told me that was the right thing to do. If I didn't know who I am talking to I should say nothing. He told me he was part of a group of half a dozen doctors who did underground work. They thought I was endangering all of them by acting so openly. He did not want me to stop, but told me I had better hide in the shadows if I wanted to continue. We talked for about half an hour. He gave me pointers on how to avoid video surveillance, how not to attract attention. The best way was to avoid the security cameras altogether. That was becoming more and more difficult. A lot of the cameras were old so they had poor resolution in low light. He told me what kind of markers video surveillance teams used to characterize suspicious behavior. We discussed the use of disguises. He suggested simple things like hats that could be pulled down low to hide the face. Coats and jackets should be simple, common, and nondescript. He told me not to forget the shoes. Wearing the same shoes all the time would be a give away.

"I asked him why I should go to all this trouble. That was when he told me that the Office of Program Integrity and Enforcement was cracking down on all underground activity. One of his friends had been arrested. He had spent time in jail. His house was searched, his wife harassed. His accounts were frozen. Supposedly, they had even ejected some of his underground patients from the system as a warning to other patients who might seek underground care. He didn't think that would matter. Too many people were fed up with the system and wanted a choice.

"When we finished he wished me luck, opened the door, and told me to gather my things and leave the building right away. On the way I home I wondered what had I gotten myself into. I remembered that I had nothing to lose. This might be fun.

"I became a rat. I would only make rounds at night. I knew every back alley and every abandoned building. I put away my doctor's bag. I still carried a bag with me, but now I carried bags inside bags so I could change bags several times a night. I also carried a change of clothes. I hunted around and found spots where I could leave a cache of goods in case I needed them. I got to know the night people and the homeless. I was often in a position to help them and they would help me. I had spent the past few years walking everywhere at all hours so I was a familiar sight and even the police merely waved.

"I started out trying to stay in the shadows, but that was never going to be good enough. I spent months charting the locations of security cameras. I started out doing this by observation, but the son of one of my patients told me of a device that scans for video cameras. I could never afford one. He got one for me which made my plot of video cameras go a lot quicker.

"Over the years several other underground doctors have introduced themselves. We don't talk for long and never in the open. One day I was contacted by someone offering to supply medications. I thought it was a set up so I didn't bother to respond. The next time I met with one of the other underground doctors I asked him if he knew this would be supplier. He told me the supplier was legitimate. The supplier somehow gets his hands on some recently expired meds and donates them to the cause. That's how he put it, the cause. I was always looking for ways to do more for my people. I told this underground doctor that if he ran into the supplier to tell him I would be interested. One day I was sitting in the park reading a book. Someone said, 'Take care, Doc,' and when I got back to my apartment I found a collection of meds in my bag.

"With this I was entering new territory. Before I was just a former doctor offering advice and kindness. The medications were clearly contraband. Possession was probably a criminal offense. I moved them out of the apartment the same night and scattered them in safe spots around the city.

"This new life, these new precautions became routine after awhile. I probably got careless. One night I was convinced I was being followed. I abandoned my usual course and took evasive measures. I lost my tail when I ducked into a building and changed clothes. I walked right past him and he didn't recognize me.

"This went on for a few nights. Always the same person followed me. He would pick me up as I left by the rear entrance to my apartment building. I always lost him by ducking into a building and changing into a disguise. It was too easy. Who was he? Was he working for someone? Was he a naked tail that I was supposed to spot and outwit so the rest of his team could follow me?

"I talked this over with some friends. They wanted to take him prisoner and, shall we say, interrogate him. I couldn't have that. We came up with another plan.

"The next night I went out as I usually did. I spent more time than usual doubling back and going in circles, but I never tried to lose him until I brought him to a section of town where my friends were set up. I did my quick change into a disguise and left him to my friends.

"Soon after I lost him he made a phone call. We were set up with an interceptor so we could listen in on his call. It was clear that he was part of a larger organization, but which one? My friends followed him back to his car. It was an official car with government plates. We ran the plates through the computer and OPIE came up.

"This was not good. OPIE never used one agent when they could use ten. I could only conclude that I was supposed to discover the tail. Was I being followed by a team of agents that I never saw? Or was this a form of intimidation?

"The next day a friend came and swept my apartment for bugs. There was one, only one, but that would be enough.

"My first thought was to ignore it, but when OPIE realized I was not going to lead them to any of the other underground doctors I would be picked up. It is not that I fear incarceration, but it would be the end of my work. The next day I walked away. I have no place I can call home now. All I have is my work and my friends.

"Still, OPIE tries to hunt me down. To them I am a ghost. Rumors reach them. No matter how hard they try they haven't been able to get anything solid, but the Director will never give up."

He stopped. I had gotten so used to the rhythm of his speech that it took me a moment to realize it. "Can you tell me anything about other underground doctors?" I asked him.

"Not much," he said. "There are others. Most are doctors entirely outside the system. Some are like me, doing the work for the joy of the work, but there are others who are paid for their work."

"How about this character that supplies you with medications? Can you tell me anything about him?"

"I know precious little about him and I cannot reveal even that."

"Can you tell me how you live now that you don't have a home?"

"I have a lot of friends. To tell you more would be like telling the Director where to find me."

"The Director, then, you said you knew her."

"Ah, yes, the high priestess, beauty and the beast all rolled into one. She worked at the clinic for awhile. I met her a few times. She acted as if she expected to be the center of attention any time she walked into a room. She had probably gotten a lot of free passes in life. I remember wondering how someone so beautiful had ended up a doctor, but then I learned her father was a doctor. She only lasted a couple of years. She couldn't stand seeing patients so she left to take a job with OPIE. The next time I saw her was when she put an end to my first underground practice. She had risen fast in OPIE, an assistant director in just a few years. She was still beautiful, but there was this strange intensity about her. She looked at me with those unnaturally blue eyes and I was afraid. At the time I put it off on my being worried about my wife's transplant. Since then my life has bumped into the Director's more than once. I've thought back to that day. She's become a scourge harassing people who are desperate for something the system can't or won't provide and people who are just trying to care. The Director has an unshakeable belief that she is right and is more than willing to destroy anyone who disagrees with her. You are attracted to her beauty only to find yourself trapped. How about you? You must have met the Director."

"Only twice," I told him. "Once was at night in a dark parking lot. The other was in her office with the sun setting right behind her. Neither time could I get a good look at her so I was surprised when you said she was beautiful. She set me up so I didn't have a choice. It ruined my life. I knew I was being watched, first by her and then by you. I'd go out for a beer with my buddies and spend the evening scanning the room trying to figure out who was there to watch me. In the end I hesitated to make a call or to contact a friend with the computer. I was worried that I might get them into some type of trouble."

"I am sorry about that. We had to know who you were. But as to your friends you should not have bothered worrying. OPIE already knew more about you than you know yourself. So much of our lives are on computers. They are all searchable with the proper tools. The best thing is to ignore it. Act as if no one was watching. The banality of our daily existence protects us."

"I can see that now. Someone who is not making calls and not sending computer messages is acting suspiciously. In the end I had been drawn in. I had to meet this black market doctor who could dispatch henchman to do his bidding. I think I even thought I was risking my life. It was exciting. Now it all seems so ...."

"Banal?"

"Yes, I guess that fits. But it doesn't all fit together. If you never take any money, how can you employ all these people that you used to outsmart OPIE?""

"I told you. I don't employ anyone. I am blessed with many friends. I work on the principle of love."

"Yeah, love, you told me that. It is just hard to believe in today's world."

"Really? Do you think human nature has changed so much? Let me ask you this. Why do you think the Director is still here and not in Washington?"

"I did wonder why the Director that my friend called 'legendary' was not at the main office in D.C."

"There may be other reasons, but I like to think the reason is love. The Director was married. She had a child, a beautiful little girl. About the time the child was three there was a very strange car accident killing both her husband and her child. I don't think she's ever been able to leave them."

"That's so sad."

"Even you feel sorry for her when you see her human side. Remember it. This will not end well. You will never write that story. She will see to it."

"Then why do it? Why go to all this trouble."

"Well, in some ways it is an important story, but the real reason is I'm getting old. I can't continue like this much longer. I was hoping that the Director might give up this quest of hers. I'm not the problem she is after. Then there is always the possibility that I am wrong about you. Maybe you will fool me and the Director and write this story."

With that Dr. L. stood up and put on his hat and coat. "Where are you going?" I asked him.

"It is nearly dawn and I have become a creature of the night," he said.

He led the way out to the balcony. There was a ladder waiting for him. I should have expected it. "Here, give me a hand," he said while climbing over the railing. "I'm not as nimble as I once was."

When he was on the ladder he held out his hand and I took it. "Good luck, Justin, you are going to need it."

"I'm going to surprise you, Dr. L. I'm going to write that story."

"I hope so." He took a step down the ladder. "Wait. I almost forgot this." He reached into his pocket, pulled out a small metal box, and handed it to me.

"This is yours," he said, "but don't open it until I am gone. OPIE will know where you are the second you open it. They have used it the whole time to keep track of you. If you have a number to call I would call it immediately. They will show up here in any case and at least you will look cooperative." He looked around at the lightening sky. "Dawn, July 4th, a new Independence Day, let's see what you can do with it."

I watched him climb down the ladder. A car without any lights drove up. He entered with a last wave and the car disappeared into the night. Stepping back into the hotel room I opened the box. Inside was an object wrapped in metal foil. It was my GPS watch. I hadn't even noticed it was missing.

Remembering what Dr. L. had said I put the battery back in my hand held computer and made the call. Then I sat down to wait. A lot of what Dr. L. said flashed through my brain. If the Director wanted to prevent my writing the story she might confiscate my recorders. I rewound both and listened. Both had gotten the tail end of the interview so I presumed both had worked throughout. I took one and wrapped it in the metal foil. After placing it in the metal box I stepped outside on the balcony. The light was dim, but I couldn't be sure that the surveillance camera hadn't been turned on now that Dr. L. had left. I leaned against the side of the balcony. There was a bush a few feet to the side. I tried to casually drop the box. I saw it disappear into the bush.

Inside the hotel room I thought about my notes. I hadn't taken many notes because I had the recorders. The Director was bound to confiscate my notes and I wanted to keep the few I had. There would be no way to hide anything in the hotel room even if I could make a copy. I decided to send a voice message to my office number.

I was near the end when I heard the door open. I ended the call, straightened my papers, and looked up. My first thought on seeing the Director was, "This isn't going to be too bad." When she stepped into the room she stopped, posed really, just a few seconds for effect. It was quite an effect. Dr. L. had called her beautiful. He was not doing her justice. I had expected some averagely attractive middle aged woman. Here was a beauty queen perfectly turned out. I can still see her as she stood there. She wore three inch heels and a suit with the skirt cut an inch or two too high. Under the jacket was a cream colored blouse cut way too low and around her neck was a necklace with a large pendant that fell to the level of her blouse. Her makeup and hair were perfect.

I knew she was in her fifties, but she did not look over forty. I now know the discipline that takes, the hours in the gym, the dieting, the shots, the surgery. Most of us just don't care that much. You have to be driven. If I had known that then I might have had the sense not to relax. Instead I sat there and scoped her up and down just as she stood there knowing I would do just that.

I imagine there are women and, perhaps, even men who might think this debasing, but they should think about it. Her beauty was a weapon. I had been in her presence twice before and had no clue. Tonight she wanted a weapon. Of course, she may have dressed this way because she expected to take Dr. L. into custody or she came from a night out. The way she dressed may not have had anything to do with me, but consider what happened next. She smiled. I smiled. In a pleasant almost sexy voice she said, "Mr. Lodge." I started to stand. She strides over saying, "Please, don't stand on my account," and pushes me back in the chair. Then she leans over with her eyes just a few inches from mine where I have to look into those blue eyes and she rips me a new one with that command voice containing a hint of sarcasm that I heard in her office.

I start to look away from those eyes, but looking down I'm looking down her blouse. That would never do. If I look away entirely she knows she has won so I concentrate on those blue eyes remembering what Dr. L. told me. This is a woman who lost her husband and child, who lost everything she loved in the world.

Finally, the Director stepped back. The spell was broken. "Don't expect to get paid for this. And I want your recording of the interview."

I don't know whether it was the tongue lashing I just received or the mention of money, but I snapped. I jumped to my feet and stood over her as much as someone six-one can stand over someone five-eight in three inch heels. We went at it. "If you don't pay you're not getting the recording." Not that I cared about the money.

"Your mission failed."

"My mission was to get an interview. You're the people who let an old man outsmart them."

"He got to you, didn't he? It doesn't matter. I can't let you out of here with that recording. It is evidence in an ongoing investigation. Maybe you'd like an obstruction of justice charge?"

"You know I just don't care anymore. Do whatever you have to do."

"Maybe we'll throw in aiding and abetting a known felon."

"Dr. L., a felon? You people have your heads up your asses. Avoiding OPIE is probably more excitement than he's had in his life."

"What did he give you, that holier than thou 'I'm only out to help people' crap? You have no idea how dangerous he is? How many people he's injured?"

"I don't care. You're not getting the recording."

At this the Director took her bag off her shoulder, pulled out a gun, and pointed at me. "I can't let you leave with that recording."

The gun brought me up short. I wasn't familiar with guns and I never had one pointed at me. But I just didn't care. I pushed past her. "You'll never shoot me over a recording."

She shot the door over my head just before I reached it. You never want to hear a gun go off in an enclosed space pointed in your general direction. I certainly did not want to hear it again. The Director and I had been playing chicken and she won. "Okay, okay," I said, "you win." I reached into my pocket for the micro-recorder, but before I took it out I pressed the erase button.

The Director took the recorder out of my hand. Two agents from OPIE burst into the room. "Search him and search the room. Confiscate anything that might be evidence."

"Right, Director. Do we take him into custody?"

The Director looked me up and down. With a shake of her head she said, "Don't bother. He'll be easy to pick up if we need him." Then we all watched her glide from the room.

# Part Three

I should never have erased the interview. The Director was going to be angry when she found out. I was sure she would have me picked up. I did not want to have the recording around when the agents came. They were bound to search the apartment then my act of defiance would be wasted. When a week had passed and I still had my freedom I began to wonder if I had erased the interview.

I went back to the hotel. Remembering the advice of Dr. L., I borrowed clothes from a friend, even shoes, so I would not be seen wearing anything that could be identified with me. I wore a hat and sunglasses as well as a clip-on earring. I let my beard grow. I even left behind my hand held computer and my GPS watch. I had a friend drop me miles away. I spent time in a couple of fast food spots paying cash. When I got to the hotel I worked my way around the outside looking in all the bushes. I had dropped the box in a bush near the back entrance.

The box was there. I palmed it a nonchalantly as I could. I continued with my search around the building half expecting security to scare me away at any minute.

Back at the apartment I broke open a speaker and inserted the box. I didn't even bother to listen to the recording. I was not ready. The Director had shaken me when she called Dr. L. a felon. What did I really know? Perhaps he had broken the law in a way more serious than just giving advice. Maybe he had caused someone's death.

I decided to look up Dr. L. on the computer. I made the assumption that the 'L' was a real initial. He was a family practitioner and the son of a family practitioner in the same city where he had lived his whole life. He had worked for one of the local clinics and he must be in his 70's. I didn't think it would be too hard.

I found his father first. Daniel Love's obituary was in a local on-line paper 15 years ago. He practiced family medicine at the same address for forty years, the last decade with his son, Donald. There followed a long list of groups he had been a member of and all the times he had been president of this or that.

Two years earlier there was a nice article on Dr. L. in the on-line newsletter of the city medical society. Donald Love was doctor of the year. Whoever wrote it had a high regard for Dr. L. I could just see the father sitting in the audience, so proud of his son. On the next page was a picture of a younger version of Dr. L. I felt a little better. I found it hard to believe that a 'doctor of the year' could be a felon. I kept searching. I even paid for a background check. I found nothing suggesting Dr. L. was a felon.

I still was not ready to write about the underground doctor. I would sit with my friends watching a game. My eyes would take in the speaker where I had hidden the box. I needed to be certain to give the story what it needed. I needed more information.

I decided to work on the other side of the equation. I searched OPIE and the Director. When I wrote the article on OPIE closing the clinic I had scanned the OPIE website. The website had been a bore. This time was not much better. There was the all important mission statement, a list of all regional and local offices with telephone numbers, and a short bio of the director of the whole operation in Washington. There was no mention of Director Stricker. On the other hand I did have a number to call for employment opportunities with OPIE.

I narrowed my search to see if I could come up with something on Director Stricker. The only item I found that was pertinent was my own on-line article. I did find a lot of Strickers. The first few articles started to round out the picture. They were an old family in town that owned a sizeable firm with 500 to 1000 employees, mostly engineering, but over the years had morphed into electronics and computers. There were several articles announcing the awarding of contracts from the government including one from OPIE. It was all very interesting, but not what I was after.

I kept going back page by page. The reference I was looking for had to be there. Finally I found the obituary for John Stricker. He died in a car accident along with his four year old daughter Deidre. He was survived by his wife, Dr. April Stricker. I had a first name now.

The next page on my search had a featured article on the car accident. There was an eyewitness report by someone trailing the car on the expressway. The car was sailing along going just over the speed limit without any hint of a problem when it suddenly spun out, hit the railing, and exploded. The picture from the scene showed not much more than a frame left after the explosion. At that time it was probably a gas guzzler, but I could not believe that a gas tank explosion had done that much damage.

I paged back and forth looking for follow-up on the accident. I could not find a reference. I started paging back in time for the article I knew was there. After another ten pages I found the wedding announcement for April Anne Love and John Forrest Stricker. That's right, April Anne Love. Where the heck did that come from?

Searching back another year I found the engagement announcement. There was a close-up of the happy couple. John Forrest was handsome, but April Anne was....

I must have sat there staring at that picture for five minutes, looking at those eyes I had seen from six inches away, those eyes that had tried to burn a hole through my brain, and trying to connect it with that smile so innocent, so sweet, so hopeful.

I woke up, dropped the computer on the couch, and went into the kitchen for a beer. I drank it down and grabbed another. I stood in the doorway to the kitchen staring at the computer. I did not want to go back there and stare at those eyes again. I did not want my life sucked down this drain, but I couldn't let it go.

One of my roommates, Tom, came in, sat on the couch, and picked up the computer. "Wow, who's the babe?" he asked.

"The local director of OPIE."

"OPIE? What's that?"

I forgot that no one had ever heard of OPIE. "The Office of Program Integrity and Enforcement, has to do with healthcare. It's that federal agency thing I wrote about a few months ago."

"Yeah, she looks kind of young to be a director."

"The picture was taken over thirty years ago."

"Too bad, she still look this good?"

"Older, but, yeah, she still looks that good."

"Mind if I look up some ball scores?"

Tom had already switched screens so I just turned back to the kitchen to find something to eat. His voice reached me through the door. "We got a game in half an hour. You coming?" I heard him say. I don't know why he asked. I always did.

The next day I was back at the computer. The Director's father was Joseph Love, a cardio-thoracic surgeon in the Chicago area. The only thing I could find of interest was that Joseph Love was in his mid-fifties when the Director was born. Her mother was Victoria Landfelt aged twenty-five when the Director was born. Her father had died twenty years ago.

I went to several websites for genealogy and inserted all the names I knew. I could not make a connection between April Anne Love and Donald Love. I had one more item I wanted to clear up.

The next weekend I was standing in front of the graves of John Forrest Stricker and Deidre Victoria Stricker. There were fresh flowers. The graves were in the Stricker section of the cemetery. None of the other graves had flowers. It was not near a birth date or the date of the accident. Someone must care.

I thought of staking out the cemetery to see if the Director would come, but what would be the point. I had not heard from OPIE since the night of the interview. I was hoping they would forget about me. If the Director caught me snooping I don't know what she might do.

In the end I decided to take Dr. L's advice, act as if nothing is happening, let the banality of my existence deflect any attention. I went back to beer and ballgames with my buddies, I talked to my friends as if no one were listening, I sent text messages as if no one other than its intended recipient would ever read them, but I still noted the surveillance cameras, I still watched over my shoulder to see if I was being followed.

One night something happened that changed my life. I was in the bar I usually go to with my friends. We were standing at the bar waiting for a table to open. I heard a laugh. I turned to find out who had made that noise. At the other end of the bar there was a small group of two guys, three girls. One of the girls caught my attention as being the source of the laugh. She had short, dark hair that seemed casually blown around her face. She was having more fun than anyone else in the room. With her movements, her smile, her laugh, she was more alive than anyone else in the room.

I was captivated. Everything else just dropped away. I found myself wondering if she was paired up with one of the others. I don't know how long I stared, but finally one of the other girls noticed. She elbowed the girl with the dark hair and smile. They both stuck out their tongues at me. They laughed, I laughed, and we all turned away.

A couple of hours later I was sitting at a table by myself. My friends had left me to play pool. Normally I would have joined them, but not that night. I had kept track of the girl with the dark hair for most of the night. The last half hour or so I had not seen her. I thought she and her friends had left. Suddenly she slid into the chair across from me, leaned forward, and asked, "Was it good for you?"

Not being prepared all I got out was, "What?"

"That staring thing at the bar, I hope you enjoyed it."

I leaned back trying to come up with some sarcastic come back. The thought occurred to me that it must have taken some courage to come over here. Instead of making a crushing remark that I would later regret I leaned forward, put out my hand, and said, "My name is Justin. Would you go out with me sometime?"

She took my hand. Her smile got even bigger. "My name is Tif. What's wrong with now?"

Tif was short for Tiffany. We left the bar and found some place we could talk over coffee and pie. We moved in together three months later. Tif was a couple of years older than I was. She had a wild, mischievous side that made her more fun to be with than anyone I knew. Every weekday morning she would leave for her job in a bank all prim and proper as if the wild woman did not exist. She worked in the audit department at the bank, but she really was a writer. A few of her stories had shown up in on-line magazines. More of her stories were published in the underground newspapers that were making a comeback as people got tired of the censorship on the web. She was half way through a novel. Neither of us knew what the point of writing a novel was in today's world, but if you are a writer you write. Practicality did not play a part.

The amazing thing was that I was actually writing, nothing big, but at least I was stringing words together again. I think the problem was that when I lived with my friends I never felt comfortable talking about my writing. With Tif we talked writing all the time.

Life was good and simple. I went to work and came home to Tif. OPIE, the Director, and Dr. L. were distant memories. I stopped looking over my shoulder and I was too busy looking into Tif's eye to notice the surveillance cameras. Then the pains began.

I woke up one night with a sharp pain on the left side of my abdomen. I got out of bed and went into the living room. I ended up lying down on the couch with my feet up. The pain stopped a couple of hours later. After a couple of more episodes Tif convinced me to go to the clinic.

The last time I used the health care system was when I broke a bone playing football in high school. Tif sat with me while I signed in with the secretary. The secretary asked the usual identifying questions. She got a funny look on her face, asked the questions again, shook her head. She asked for photo ID. She typed rapidly into the system, shook her head again. "You are a citizen, aren't you?"

"Of course," I told her. "Why? What's the problem?"

"I can't find you in the system. The only time I've seen that has been with a non-citizen. You say it has been a decade since you accessed the healthcare system? I'm sure that is the problem. Your personal health record should clear everything up."

I don't know why she didn't ask for that right off. Trying to access the healthcare system without your personal health record is punishable with a fine of up to $5000. Everybody carried it with them at all times usually as a necklace around there neck. I unclipped my personal healthcare record and handed it over.

The secretary plugged my personal record into the computer. She shook her head again. "I'm afraid when I plugged your record into the computer I got an alert telling me that this record has been reported stolen. I'm to call security immediately."

The secretary put her hand over the microphone she wore and mouthed the word, "Run."

Tif and I were stunned. Neither of us moved until she picked up the phone and said, "Security?"

Tif and I ran out of the building. On the way home to our apartment it hit me. This was the Director's revenge. I'd been ejected from the system for erasing the interview. I told Tif the whole story about my interview with an underground doctor. "Don't worry," she told me, "now your just one of us."

"What do you mean?"

"Have you ever seen my personal health record?"

"Darling, I've seen every inch of you."

"Yes, you have, but you've never seen my personal health record because I don't have one."

"I always thought you just didn't like to wear it to bed or maybe you kept it in a wallet. Some people don't like to wear it around their neck or wrist all the time. I thought you were just being different."

"You thought wrong. My parents are refuseniks."

"Refuseniks?"

"Yes, refuseniks were an oppressed minority in the Soviet Union. When people started refusing to use mainstream medicine to keep their health information out of the government data base they borrowed the name."

"So, you're telling me that you've never seen a regular doctor."

"They were all regular doctors. They just didn't include us in the computer. It wasn't such a big deal at first. Now it is a big deal. You can be fined for not having a personal health record. It rarely occurs, but the threat is there. Doctors caught giving undocumented care, that's the term they use for anything that is not in the federal data base, face being imprisoned. It is even worse if they are trying some new unapproved therapy even if that therapy is routine in another country."

"Don't you need a health record for school and work?"

"Luckily there's a law against employers even asking about the personal health record. As far as school goes I was home schooled through high school and there are some colleges that don't require a personal health record."

"Geesh, I guess there's a whole world out there I knew nothing about and now I'm part of that world whether I like it or not."

Tif told me not to worry, these things work out, but it almost didn't. The next week the pain came in the middle of the night. When the pain did not go away I called in sick. By the time Tif came home after work I was very sick. I was in severe pain, I could not keep anything down, and I had a fever.

I had made up my mind to go to the hospital and accept the consequences of not having my personal health record. Tif told me that there was someone who might help, but she was going to have to leave me alone for awhile. A couple of long hours later she came home alone. "If nobody shows in the next hour," she told me, "I'll take you to the hospital."

The next hour felt like three. I was ready to give up when there was a knock at the door. Tif came in with Dr. L. The first thing he did was turn on some music while Tif closed all the blinds.

"Mr. Lodge, I hear you've gotten yourself into a bit of a problem."

"Dr. L.," I called him Dr. L. I knew his name, but I couldn't bring myself to use it. "I didn't expect to see you again."

"Nor I you, but Tif's family are old friends. Why don't you tell me how it all started?"

"It started about six weeks ago. I woke up with this severe pain on the left side of my abdomen that seemed to go down into my leg. It lasted two to three hours. Then it went away. I'd feel fine for a few days, maybe a week. Then it would come back again, last for a few hours, and go away. This time the pain came and hasn't gone away for more than a day. I can't keep anything down, I have a fever and chills, and the pain is worse than before. Anytime I sit up I feel like I'm going to pass out."

"Just lie there, then, and let me examine you."

Dr. L. took out some device and wrapped it around my wrist. After he pressed a button it got tight. He checked the reading and repeated the process a couple of times before trying the other wrist. He looked in my throat. He listened to my heart and lungs. When he poked my abdomen it felt like a hot knife. As he went he continued to ask questions.

When he finished Dr. L. stowed his equipment and said, "You need to get yourself to the nearest hospital emergency room as soon as possible."

I could not believe Dr. L. was telling me that. "No, I won't go. Isn't there something you can do?"

"Listen. I think you have a kidney stone. You probably have been passing small stones for awhile. Now you have one that is stuck and your kidney is infected. It is a little unusual to get an infection so soon, but it is the only thing that explains the fever and chills. Between the fever and not being able to keep anything down you are dehydrated. You need intravenous fluids and antibiotics as well as doing something about the stone. If you go to an emergency room they will take care of you."

"No," I told him, "I can't do that. I'll end up in jail."

Dr. L. shook his head. "Because of being ejected from the system? I doubt it. You probably will go through a rough few months, but you have done nothing wrong. You will undergo a lot of questioning. You cannot tell them about this visit and, of course, Tif might be a problem. She is in the system, but has not accessed it for so long that it might raise a flag or two. I would probably suggest you two break up for a bit, just until this blows over. You do know that if they really wanted to they would know all about you two. When you went to the clinic the computer undoubtedly advised OPIE of your attempt to sign in. They would get a picture of Tif off the surveillance cameras. It is not too hard to identify her through facial recognition then they can apply all their electronic search techniques and develop an amazingly complete file. Chances are they have not bothered. The Director is just trying to punish you for your act of defiance. She will make you sweat, but in the end someone in OPIE will call the prosecutor's office and explain that there has been some computer error. You will even get a new personal health record."

"You sound as if you trust the Director."

"I do. I don't think the Director is evil. I just think she is wrong based on a misapprehension of the world."

"Just how long have you known April Anne, Doctor?"

"Ah, I see you have been doing your homework. Someday we will talk about April Anne, but today you have to decide. Will you go to the hospital or won't you?"

I was having trouble keeping it together. Mentally I was drifting in and out. The pain was coming in spasms and was so severe I wasn't sure passing out would nor been an improvement. I saw Dr. L. waiting patiently. Behind him stood Tif biting her lip, eyes wet. Where was the smile I had fallen in love with?

I closed my eyes. I did not want to make the choice. Dr. L. had told me he always recommended patients get back into the system if they could. This was no different except I had the Director waiting for me and I was dragging Tif into it. Even with the kind words from Dr. L. I did not trust the Director. I had looked into those eyes. She would have no problem destroying me if it served her purpose. I also did not believe the Director had forgotten about me. For awhile I had forgotten about her, but with the alert at the clinic I fell back into her trap. She would have me under surveillance again.

"Dr. Love, isn't there something you can do?" It was Tif.

"Yes, there is, but Justin needs to decide."

"I'm sorry to have gotten you involved in this, Tif," I said. "If I had any idea…."

"Don't worry about me. My family has been underground for a long time so I'm used to it. What do you want to do?"

"I don't want to go crawling back to the Director. If there is anything I can do other than go to the hospital I will do it."

Dr. L. stood up. "That's what I thought you would say. I've already started the process. But let me tell you this, what you are about to do is not illegal. The risk is entirely on the side of the providers of care. These men and women will be risking their careers and, perhaps, their freedom. Never forget that. We will have to take a lot of precautions and we may have to turn back. Now, meet me at the backdoor in twenty minutes. I'll send someone up to help you down. Wear long coats with the collars turned up, hats pulled low, and sunglasses if you have them, anything to avoid facial recognition, take off all your jewelry including rings, and leave anything electronic at home."

I watched Dr. L. walk out. Looking up at Tif I said, "I'm sorry." All she did was kiss me.

Ten minutes later there was a knock on the door. A rather large gentleman entered the apartment. He held a finger up to his lips. Without saying a word he pulled me off the coach and helped me into a coat. He carried me out of the apartment where he indicated for Tif to take the stairs while we took the elevator. At the backdoor he deposited me in the back seat of an old gas guzzler. Tif slid into the front seat a minute later. Dr. L. drove off.

I was lying down in the back so I depended on Dr. L. and Tif to keep me informed.

"How are you doing back there?" Dr. L. asked.

"Moving around has made the pain worse."

"Hopefully, it will settle down. We found a micro-camera trained on the backdoor of your apartment, definitely not placed there by building management so we will have to take some precautions. Let's find a block to drive around."

My body felt the car take a few corners. "I'm afraid we are being followed, although it may just be my paranoia. Let me try going around another block. Tif, if you could turn around and watch through the rear window that way you can keep an eye on whoever is following us and our patient at the same time.

I felt the car turn and turn again. "What do you think, Tif? Is that car behind us now following us?"

"I think so, Dr. L. When you changed lanes he changed lanes and then changed lanes again when you did to follow you around the corner. Two idiot drivers doing the same thing would be unusual."

"I agree. We're going to head downtown."

Over the next ten minutes Dr. L. came to a stop three times and turned twice. I started recognizing the outlines of some of the downtown buildings. "We'll turn in here," Dr. L. said and made a sharp turn coming to a stop. Dr. L. used a card to raise a gate, honked to get the attention of an attendant, gave a wave, and headed down to the lower levels. My body, exquisitely sensitive to any change in position, told me every time Dr. L. whipped the car around a corner. We jerked to a stop.

Dr. L. turned around to check on me. "Sorry about that, Justin, but we don't have much time. We have to transfer to another vehicle."

Someone was there to help Tif get me into the backseat of a van. Dr. L. switched his hat and coat with the person who had helped me into the van. I saw him drive the other car away before Dr. L. closed the door to the van.

"We'll give Ramon a head start. This parking garage has three exits. Ramon will leave by the exit we came in. Hopefully, if there are other cars following us they'll mistake Ramon for me and call the other cars. In any case we're going to head out of town on the interstate. If someone is still following us we'll just have to lose them out there."

Dr. L. started the van and whipped us back up and out of the garage with my body cringing at every turn. After that it seemed like a straight shot. I watched the high rises disappear. After another half hour the lights became less frequent. I thought we must be in farm country. Dr. L. and Tif were chatting away up front while I was just trying to stay conscious in back. The car slowed to a stop. I could see the interstate above us. We just sat there. "Why aren't we moving?" I asked.

"Probably just my paranoia, but I thought I saw a car following us. I pulled off, but I haven't seen that car drive by on the interstate. I might have missed it, but I think it stopped just at the beginning of the exit ramp with its lights off."

"So, what do we do?"

"I'm going to drive off into the countryside for about a mile, find someplace to turn around quickly, and see if they follow."

Dr. L. did just that. He told me to hold on when he whipped it through a one-eighty. It still hurt. Lights passed us going the other way. "I can't be sure, but I think that was the car from the interstate. I don't plan on waiting around to find out." Dr. L. gunned it and headed for the interstate.

After we were on the interstate for awhile DR. L. said, "There's a car coming, must be doing 90. I'm going to slow down and see if he passes."

A few minutes later Dr. L. said, "He's slowed down and keeping his distance. Perhaps it's time to get some gas."

I felt the van slow down and change direction. A minute later we were stopped at a gas station. Dr. L. said, "You know, this is a special van. It is a true hybrid. The driver can change from electronic to gas drive. Even when driving electronically there is no stable electronic signature to lock onto. The gas drive is shielded so it has a minimal infrared signature. I've tried all variations since we left the parking garage and they seem to find us at will. Are you sure neither of you has anything electronic on you? Check your wallets. Some of the newer identity cards have chips in them that can be traced."

Tif said, "I left everything at home. I didn't even bring a wallet. I know Justin didn't bring anything, but what about that watch?"

"Oh, crap! I'm sorry, Dr. L. I forgot all about my GPS watch. I'm sorry."

"It's not your fault, son. You are so sick you are barely conscious. I knew about it. I should have thought of it. Now let me have that watch and let's see if we can have some fun. Tiffany, why don't you look in that first aid kit and see if there is some tape or band aids."

"Both tape and band aids."

"Tear off a couple of strips of tape. You take the watch and go for a walk out to the road and back. Bend over and stretch a couple of times. When you come back bend over like your stretching behind that car. Try to attach the watch to the car. It doesn't have to be permanent. If it stays attached for five or ten minutes we'll be good. I'm going to talk to the driver and divert his attention."

Dr. L. and Tif got out of the van. A few minutes later Tif and Dr. L. got back in. "Were you able to get the watch attached?"

"Yes. I wedged it behind the license plate then taped it."

"Good. What we're going to do is follow this fellow when he leaves for about a mile then we are going to look for some place to pull off where we can wait with our lights off. Hopefully, whoever is following us will follow the watch. When they drive by we will head the other way."

Dr. L. started the van. We waited. "Here we go," Dr. L. said and I felt the van move.

We drove along for about two minutes until Dr. L. said to Tif, "We lucked out. The car you attached the watch to did not get back on the interstate. Start looking for a driveway or road off to the side. We can't take a chance on our pursuers catching up to us before we turn off and we have to get far enough off the road that they won't see us."

"There."

"Yes, I see it."

The van slowed and we made a turn. Dr. L. turned all the lights off. "We'll watch out the back window to see if our pursuers are chasing the watch. They shouldn't be more than two or three minutes behind us."

We waited in the dark. Tif saw them first.

"There they are."

"Yes, at least I hope it's them. Tiffany, why don't you go out to the road and make sure they didn't stop just up the road."

Tif got out of the car and came back a minute later. "It looks clear, Dr. Love."

"Great, then let's get out of here before they realize their mistake and double back."

Dr. L. started the van, backed into the road, and took off. "How are you doing back there, son?" he asked.

"Not too good. The chills are coming in waves. The pain is severe, but I can tolerate it until we go around a corner or make a sudden stop. I'm having trouble staying conscious. I'd like to let go, but I'm a little worried I might not wake up again."

"Sorry about that. The good thing is we don't have much further to go, that's why I had to lose them now. We were lucky they were so stupid or, perhaps, it was arrogance. Either way they should never have bothered following us as long as they could follow your watch's signal. They are so used to electronic surveillance that they get sloppy and get tripped up by some low tech counter. Most of the high tech methods they use have been around for years, but now they are so ubiquitous it is hard to escape. Add to that the fact that everything is interconnected and the increasing sophistication of search techniques it is easy to understand their arrogance. Still, losing them was almost too easy. It worries me that I've missed something, but it can't be helped now. We've wasted enough time."

In a few minutes I felt the van slow to pull off the interstate. We came to a stop. The van door opened and several people picked me up and placed me on a stretcher. I thought we must have reached our destination, but they just rolled me into the back of another van. This was all performed in a near pitch black darkness and almost without a sound. Tif got in the back next to me and found my hand.

"You're in good hands now, son. These people will take good care of you."

"Aren't you coming with us?" I heard Tif ask him.

"No. My job is to take this van a hundred miles away by morning and show up on their database by running a red light. I've never been to the facility where they are taking you. It is safer that way."

"Dr. L., thank you," I told him.

"Just get better, son. Just get better."

An attendant got in the back with us. The doors closed and I felt the van move. We were rolling for awhile when Tif asked, "Can't we put on a light?"

"No, it is for everyone's protection. The van is actually being driven without lights using night vision technology. If there is an emergency we will light up."

When you are acutely ill and every bump sends a throb of pain through your body the seconds seem like minutes. My guess is that it was thirty to forty minutes before we came to a stop and the rear doors of the van opened. I was rolled out into the dark. I guess everyone was using night vision technology. I got the feeling of a large building that smelled like a barn. I remember thinking, "Oh, my God, they've taken me to a barn. I'm going to die."

They rolled me down a ramp and into an elevator. I had the feeling of going down. The elevator opened and we had the first normal illumination since the gas station. Tif was escorted away. I did not like that because despite Dr. L's encouragement I was scared to death. I was stripped of my clothes, helped into some type of gown, and placed on a conveyor belt to pass through a wall.

The next room was brilliantly lit and all in white. I had the impression of not just clean, but sterile. A team of people dressed in greens with facemasks and hair caps transferred me to a stretcher and went to work. One started an intravenous, another hooked me up to monitors, and a third started examining me. After listening to my lungs and poking my belly the one who was examining me pulled up a machine and started running a probe over my abdomen. After a few passes she became excited. "There's the little bugger," she said. "Look at that dilation. That's gotta hurt. It is incredible the image I'm getting of the anatomy. I've got to get one of these things. Make sure we're capturing the image. I want copies for my files."

She spent another fifteen minutes examining the rest of my abdomen before she put the probe away and addressed me. "Mr. Lodge, you've got a stone stuck in your left ureter. With the amount of dilation in the proximal ureter and renal pelvis it looks like it has been there for awhile. Your kidney looks infected. There are several small stones in both renal pelvises. The rest of the abdomen looks normal with the exception of some mild ileus secondary to the stone and infection. In addition you are severely dehydrated. We're giving you intravenous fluids and antibiotics now. In a minute we're going to give you something for pain and nausea that might put you to sleep. Before we do that I want to tell you that we need to go up there with a probe and break up that stone to get it out. We can't do that until you are rehydrated, but once you are I want to do it right away. The sooner we get the kidney draining the faster you will feel better. Do you understand?"

I did understand, sort of. "Yes," I told her, "you want to operate. Do whatever you think necessary."

"Okay, give him the shot."

I felt something burn in my arm. The doctor walked away and there was Tif sitting in the corner, clothed in white, ends of her black hair sticking out from the cap, her smile hidden by a mask. That was the last thing I was sure of for the next forty-eight hours. All I remember are images of people in gowns and masks. I seemed to float in and out. Dream and reality intertwined. I was pretty sure Tif kissed me a couple of times, but it would not be the first time I had dreamed of that.

Suddenly, I was wide awake. The white walls assaulted my retinas causing me to squint. Out of the corner of my eye I saw Tif sitting next to my bed reading.

"Don't say it hasn't been interesting," I said.

"Justin," she said and leaped to my side.

"Yeah, I think I'm in here."

"You had me so worried when you didn't wake-up right away. They assured me you were fine, just a combination of the effects of dehydration, fatigue, and the medicines they were giving you."

"How long have we been here?"

"Just over two days, I think. Most of the first day was taken up with dealing with your dehydration and getting your electrolytes stable. How do you feel now?"

"Not bad. A little sore, but nothing like the pain I was having when we arrived. I'm hungry. I guess that's a good sign. You know I dreamed you kissed me."

"That was no dream, silly. The only time I have had this mask off was to kiss you, eat, and drink. This is an incredible place. I got the feeling I wasn't supposed to wander around so I haven't tried, but I think it is a lot bigger than what I've seen."

Someone entered the room with a tray. "Mr. Lodge, you're awake just in time. How are you?"

"Hungry."

"Good. We'll start with what's on this tray. If you can keep it down we'll try something more solid and take out the I.V. You're scheduled to go home tonight so don't eat too fast. We don't want your nausea and vomiting to recur."

She left us alone. "Are you going to be alright?" Tif asked.

"I guess I'll have to be."

We left in the middle of the night in one of their anonymous black vans. They didn't blindfold us, but it was too dark to tell much about where we had been. The driver was masked. We were given different hats, sun glasses, and coats. The driver did not go directly back to town. I think he drove around to approach town from the other side. In the early morning, just before sunrise, he left us a few blocks from our apartment.

A couple of days later I felt well enough to go back to work. I thought there was going to be all sorts of problems missing work for a few days, but someone had called in with an excuse. Same thing happened with Tif.

The next night there was a knock on our door when we were about to go to bed. Tif went to the door. When she came back she closed the blinds and turned up the sound. "You have a visitor."

Dr. L. walked in and took off his disguise. "How's the patient?"

"Not 100 per cent yet, but getting there. How come you didn't mention any of this when we did our interview?"

"Well, I was telling you about me. What I do is rather mundane. I just try to help people. I rarely do something like I did for you. I am strictly small time. I've never even been to the facility where you were treated. Part of me would like to see it, but I know it is safer for security reasons. I do know a few things about it. Supposedly it was built by a billionaire who got angry when a member of his family died at a local hospital. He wanted some place that practiced excellence. He tried to build a hospital, but there was a lot of government red tape and any place he tried to build all the local hospitals complained even though he promised the facility would only do advanced procedures not available elsewhere."

"But don't all hospitals have to be excellent? I thought that the government monitored them."

"Yes, the government does monitor them. In fact, our old friend OPIE is the monitor. The question becomes what definition of excellence you use. I will get to that, but let me finish my story. I believe the facility was built on a farm several stories beneath the barn. The barn can be used to mask many activities, but the main factor was the ability of a farm to generate electricity by various means. Any facility using a large amount of energy from the power grid would stand out as an anomaly. You were treated by some of the best doctors in the country. All the medical personnel are volunteers. As far as I know the only paid employees are the security staff. The security staff is like some secret brotherhood so I don't know much about them and don't want to.

"Why would some of the best doctors in country risk their careers without getting paid? That's an interesting story that is still being hotly debated. After the healthcare reform bill was passed the politics went back and forth for years. In some ways the politics were just window dressing for voters because both sides wanted to reign in the costs of healthcare. Over the next decade or so what developed is what I call generic care. Generic care is pretty good care. A lot of relatively new drugs came off patent and you can make people healthier with exercise, diet, and smoking cessation.

"The problems were, as they always are, with the rules that developed and their application. For example, someone, somewhere defined value as each year of life lost prior to 75 as opposed to the predicted increase in longevity. Doesn't sound like a big difference, but it is huge. Suppose you have a new drug that if taken for twenty years is predicted to increase life expectancy from 86 to 87. When we consider the tens of millions of people who might end up on the drug a year of life is huge, but by definition we have decided it has no value. When we consider the cost of the new drug there is no way it can ever be approved.

"The same equation holds true for acute illness. If you were 80 you would not have the same options as a 50 year old. This presented several problems. Some treatments such as renal dialysis would not be covered after a certain age. The policy experts who decided that hid behind the idea that it was just an insurance issue, but to the patients concerned it was a matter of life and death. Then there was the trial bar. They correctly asked why everything wasn't being done for some individuals. In the end in terms of malpractice it was safer not to have some newer treatments available than to be seen withholding them.

"I think the worst thing I saw was the change in my fellow doctors. I grew up in the era when we did everything for each patient. If the patient was going to die it was not going to be our decision, but God's. Yes, I saw some futile care, but most of it was do to poor judgment or even fear of using judgment on the part of the doctors, that and fear of malpractice. One day I ran into a doctor who had taken care of one of my old patients. He had become acutely ill and I had sent him to the hospital for admission. He died so when I ran into the doctor who took care of him I asked what had happened. The answer was that he was 82. I asked a few more questions before I realized that to this doctor the only relevant information was that the patient was 82. The ethical implications of that were totally beyond this doctor. He was just responding to what he saw as the values of society and society did not value the life of this individual. I was angry at first. The patient had played golf the week before and every time he came in for an appointment he would brag about how much money he won playing poker at the nearest casino. Now I know what the doctor who took care of this patient did was just a result of the values and culture of the organization that employed him. It is awfully hard to resist the values of your employer when to do so threatens your career. I've been there and I caved so I could support my family. But the worst part is that these values are the ones demanded by the government, not the people, the government.

"The reason for all this was cost control. When you realize that a high percentage of medical costs occur in the last six months of life and we all have a last six months of life you could just see the policy wonk thinking: If only people died before that stage we could save a lot of money. We doctors have been accused in the past of playing God, but now what is the government doing?

"As you might expect there were a lot of cracks in the system. There are always people who want more or need different. A totally parallel system developed for people who were willing to pay for it. This was especially true for some of the newest treatments based on gene therapy or stem cells that were exceedingly expensive. At first no one seemed to care, but after awhile the difference in the two tiers became an embarrassment. We don't do two tiers well in this country. The general population was starting to see the difference and the huge organizations with government contracts were complaining, claiming cherry picking and the like. The response of government was increasing regulation for the safety of the people and finally with regulations that made it impossible to work for private pay. This is where OPIE came in and stepped up its enforcement. Doctors who tried to continue openly were prosecuted under tax laws, under RICO laws, and even as terrorists. Some of these prosecutions were thrown out, but most were plea bargained with a modest fine and the ability of the doctors to continue to practice medicine as long as they never practiced independently again.

"The situation with the regulations reminded me of a movie I saw once that was made about 1950. There was a family of New York policemen. The oldest brother wanted to arrest the boyfriend of his younger sister. When the other brothers asked what charge they should use the oldest brother tells them that this is New York City where you can't walk down the street without violating ten laws. If a legal system is that bad it is really a form of terror.

"Not every doctor wants to practice generic medicine. If all you want is to administer vaccinations and examine healthy patients you could be a general pediatrician, but there are doctors who live for advancing the state of the art. They need to be at the cutting edge of medicine. These are the type of doctor that took care of you. Some of them left the U.S. and see patients from the U.S. through medical tourism. Others spend most of their time working in one of the big, government sponsored organizations, but manage to treat patients underground. Your case was actually not very interesting to them, but they usually do not see someone as young as you. It was a nice change of pace.

"So, you can see that it is a matter of definition. If your definition is generic medicine applied safely and accurately you get one answer, but if you define excellence by the most advanced care available you get another. Even the term 'available' becomes a political football."

"Wow, Dr. L., that's way more than I can handle. I just want healthcare to be there if I need it."

"Then you're like everybody else. Very few people understand the implications of the choices that have been made. Many of the choices have been made under the guise of comparative effectiveness science, but the criteria on which this science is based were political decisions."

"That's enough of that. Maybe you'd like to tell me about something simpler like April Anne Love, Dr. Love."

"I wish you wouldn't do that. Dr. Love sounds like some deejay on late night radio. I always asked everyone to call me Dr. L. or Dr. Don as did my father before me."

"That still doesn't explain how you and the Director have the same last name."

Until that moment Dr. L. had been serious. Now he smiled and looked at me like I had walked into a carefully laid trap. "Haven't found a connection, have you?" he asked.

"No," I said, "I've looked everywhere. I even requested a copy of her birth certificate, but it didn't help."

"What was the writer expecting to find? Perhaps the Director is really my love child farmed out to my distant cousin Joseph so I could pursue my career. Is that it?"

"Well, you have to admit it is more romantic. It would make a better story."

"I guess it would, but the truth is far, more dreary. There is no connection that I know of. Neither my self nor my father had ever met Dr. Joseph Love. Maybe a few hundred years ago in the old country there was some connection. I've never tried to find out. To tell the truth I don't really care. When I met her she was Dr. Stricker. I didn't learn her maiden name until years later and then it was only an ironic footnote."

"C'mon, Dr. L., you must know more about the Director after all these years."

"Not really and what I do know is mostly conjecture. I met her when she started work at the clinic. She had gotten married during medical school and this was right after residency. Her husband John came

110

from a wealthy family. He was about five years older than she was. He probably thought he had found a beautiful adornment for his home and mother for his children. The thought that April Anne might want to practice medicine probably never occurred to him. April Anne, as we both know, is made of sterner stuff. I got the feeling that she has always been a little angry at the way people treated her as a beautiful object instead of as a person. Still, she was never willing to give up the advantage her beauty gave her.

"She worked at the clinic a couple of years before moving to OPIE. She was almost forty and well on her way to becoming regional director when she had her daughter. Four years later, after she had been made regional director of OPIE, her husband and daughter died in a car accident. The initial reports were suspicious, but there were no follow up reports. When someone like John Stricker, someone who is also the husband of the director of a government agency, dies under suspicious circumstances there are rumors. The most common one was that John Stricker was drunk. I have problems believing that the Director would let her husband drive drunk. What I do know is that the Director and her husband met for an early dinner with their daughter. The Director had work to do so they switched cars rather than transfer the child seat. Fifteen minutes later the car explodes."

"Are you telling me that someone tried to kill the Director?"

"No, I don't know. I never met John Stricker and didn't really know the Director back then. It is possible that she and her husband had a passionate marriage. Now as the hunted I've tried to learn a little more about the hunter. The problem is that there is very little to tell. She is the poster child for all work and no play. OPIE is not just a job for her but a crusade. She drives her agents mercilessly, but is also very loyal to them. Despite the demands she places on her agents most of them like working for her because her intensity makes what they do seem that much more important."

Dr. L. pulled out a pocket watch. "I see I've gone past my time limit. When I make a stop like this I try to limit the amount of time in case there is active surveillance. You are under surveillance, but probably just computer review which will be reported tomorrow. Hopefully my disguise will prevent the computer report, but the Director has not forgotten about you. Expect to hear from her in the near future. I hate to put this idea in your head, but you might want to consider moving. She'll keep you under surveillance as long as you live in this town."

"Isn't what she is doing against the law?"

"Video surveillance is so ubiquitous now that it is hard to tell where the law begins and ends, but in your case you gave up your rights when you agreed to become an informant and interview me."

"Dr. L., before you go could you tell me why the Director calls you a felon? Is it because of your connection with the underground facility where I was treated?"

"No, although she would love to interrogate me about that and a lot of other things mere knowledge will not make you a felon. I have attended a number of individuals just before their death. The system had nothing to offer them and my efforts were more comfort than anything else. The Director found out about one of these patients and has threatened to bring me to trial for manslaughter. There are no arrest warrants for me, but you have to remember this about the Director. She is a true believer and thinking me a felon helps maintain that belief system because what I represent is subversive to it."

Dr. L. looked at his watch again. This time he stood up and put on his disguise. "Gotta run. Have courage you two. Tif, say hello to your parents for me."

Tif saw him out. When she came back she leaned against the doorway with a half smile on her face. "Tif, I'm sorry." I told her.

"Don't worry. Meeting the Director might be fun."

Might be fun, only Tif would think meeting the Director might be fun.

Three days later on Saturday morning the buzzer went off. Feeling better I jumped up to get it. The video for the front door showed Joey in white shirt and tie wearing his OPIE jacket.

"Joey, what do you want?"

"Justin, let me up and we can talk about it."

"No, Joey. What do you want?"

"I've been sent to bring you to headquarters."

"Is this official?"

"No, strictly unofficial."

"Then why should I come?"

"Because the Director will chew my ass if I don't bring you down."

"Not my problem."

"C'mon, Justin, help me out a little."

"Joey, you're the one who got me into this mess in the first place so I don't see where I owe you anything."

"If you don't come down voluntarily today the Director will make it official. I don't think you want to go there. And you know the Director if she wants you down at headquarters eventually you'll be there."

Joey was right about that. I was just putting off the inevitable. "Doesn't the Director know it's Saturday?"

"The Director works 24/7. Besides do you really want to be pulled out of work and have to explain to your boss that you are under investigation by OPIE."

"You almost sound like you are doing me a favor."

"I am. I even have a car waiting."

"Well, how can I refuse such a kind invitation? I'll be down in a few minutes."

"Uh, Justin, she wants both of you."

I didn't answer him. Let him stew for awhile. I found Tif making lunch. "That's Joey. He wants to take both of us down to OPIE."

Tif started putting things away. "Is this official? Does he have anything formally demanding our appearance?"

"No, it is just a friendly request from the Director, but I don't like it. I don't think we should both go. This is between me and her. Chances are if I show up she'll forget about you."

"I'm going."

"But this is not your fight."

"You're my fight. Besides I want to meet the Director. I don't think it will be a big deal. Just remember what Dr. L. told us. We haven't done anything wrong."

"Strictly speaking that may not be true for me."

Tif walked to the door and grabbed a jacket. "Then you stay home. I'll go by my self." I followed her out the door.

Outside we found Joey waiting with the car. He opened the back door for Tif and slid into the front seat next to the driver. "Thanks for coming, Tif. You don't know how much this helps me with the Director."

"No problem, Joey, everyone knows you're not responsible. Must be nice having a driver, you don't even have the responsibility of driving."

"Well, I am becoming more important in OPIE." Even the driver had to stifle a laugh at that one.

At OPIE headquarters we were split up. I ended up in a small, windowless room with a few chairs and a plain table in the center. The walls were entirely blank, but I am sure the room was wired for sound and video. I expected the Director to walk through the door at any minute. I picked out a chair and waited. There was no Director. I got up and tried the door. It was locked. I sat down in one of the other chairs. Finally, someone entered and placed a bottle of water on the table.

"The Director thought you might be thirsty," he said and left.

I was thirsty. I grabbed the bottle and twisted off the cap. Suddenly I had a vision of me with a full bladder pounding on the door trying to get someone's attention. I put the bottle down without taking a sip.

I started to pace around the table. I decided to make it into a game, first clockwise, then counter clockwise, then backwards, then sideways, then hopping on one foot, then the other, then jumping with both feet together. Then I would start the whole series again. I counted every step though I probably lost count.

I was up over six thousand and jumping backwards when the Director stepped into the room. About three thousand steps ago I had decided what I was going to say when someone showed up. "I've got fifty more of these to do. As soon as I finish I'll be right with you."

The Director calmly sat down while I did fifty more backward jumps. As I completed the process I surveyed the Director. This was the beauty queen, business division, two inch heels, slightly longer skirt, blouse with high collar, hair, make-up, and nails were flawless, and utter calm. I sat down in the chair across the table from her. I was sweating from my workout. The bottle of water stood between us. The Director picked up the bottle and placed it in her bag. With the faintest hint of a smile she said, "I guess it had to be beer."

"What have you done with Tif?"

"Ah! A weakness, so pleasant to see."

The Director pulled a small computer out of her bag and switched it on. "Here is some of the surveillance photos from a night about ten days ago. I am sure you remember it well. Here is a photo at the rear of your apartment. This is undoubtedly Dr. Donald Love. This is Tiffany Gordon. The person being helped into the car is you. The name of the person helping you into the car is unknown to us, but he is known to work with Dr. Love. Here is the car entering a parking garage. Here is the van you transferred to in the parking garage stopped just off the interstate. Again, we have the same van stopped for gas. Here we have Ms. Gordon bending over behind this other car. We think she was taping your watch to the other car. After that we lost the van. We know you went for treatment to a secret facility. I want to know the location of that facility, but, most of all, I want to know how you contact Dr. Love and where he hides out."

"Go stuff your self."

"Why Mr. Lodge, I am so disappointed. I thought we might come to a meeting of the minds. I can see now that my hopes were in vain. I guess that leaves just one thing for me to do. I am going to lock up Ms. Gordon. There are several minor offenses we can use. Don't worry, Mr. Lodge. We have nothing major so she probably would not get more than ninety days. She might even get probation or she might beat the charges. Of course, she would lose her job in the bank, but that can't be helped."

The Director put away her computer. She took out the bottle of water and placed it on the table in front of me. I watched her walk to the door. When she opened it she said, "I am afraid the apartment will be a little lonely tonight, Mr. Lodge. Perhaps if you have enough beer you can forget about Ms. Gordon. You can always pick up your old life by going back to that bar. Maybe there is a playoff game on tonight. Yes, that would be perfect. Beer and a playoff game and it would be like she never existed."

"Wait!"

"Wait, Mr. Lodge? Why ever for? I thought I was stuffing my self."

"You know this is between me, you, and Dr. L. Tiffany doesn't enter into it."

"Strictly speaking that is not true. Ms. Gordon and her family are on several lists. We tend to ignore such people unless something else pops up such as her relationship with you. I would be willing to overlook that if you were to make a constructive suggestion."

"I'll tell you everything I know if you promise to leave Tiffany out of this."

The Director closed the door, walked over to the table, and sat down. With a sweet smile of innocence she said, "Cross my heart and hope to die. Will that be good enough?" She pushed the bottle of water a little closer to me.

I took several swallows from the bottle before I started. "I really don't know that much. I don't know how to contact Dr. L. and I don't know where he lives. I don't even know much about that night. I was in severe pain and dehydrated. I was just trying to stay conscious. The whole time I was lying down in the back so I couldn't tell where we were going except by what Dr. L. and Tiffany were saying. When we left the gas station we traveled for at least ten minutes, but it might have been thirty. We transferred to another vehicle at a location near the interstate. It could not have been more than two miles from the interstate. After that we were in the back of a van that was completely dark. I thought we traveled for more than thirty minutes and maybe as long as an hour. I was pretty out of it the whole time. They mentioned driving with night vision technology. When we arrived at the facility it was completely dark. We were transported underground. The facility was bright, white, and absolutely spotless. When we left we were placed in the back of a van and driven around for a few hours before being dropped a few blocks from our apartment."

The Director sat there thinking for a minute. "Unfortunately, I believe you. Dr. Love trusts very few people so I doubt you know how to contact him. I doubt he sleeps at a fixed location. As to that night the first surveillance photo shows you incapable of walking by your self. You do not appear in the succeeding photos so you were probably lying down where the camera could not see you. The people who run the facility are vey careful. Once you were in their hands they would reveal nothing to you."

"So, we're good?"

"Yes, we are good. The information you have given me will be entered into the computer data base. Sooner or later we will have enough information in the data base to narrow the search and find this facility. It is only a matter of time. But you gave me some very important information."

"What was that?"

"Who was the weak one."

"I don't understand."

"No, I don't think you would. Let me put it this way. What is a beer guzzling lay-about like you doing with a woman like Tiffany Gordon? I really got into it with her. I thought she might give in to protect her sweet Justin because it is you, not her, who has the possibility of some serious charges being filed. Did she give in? No. For an hour and a half to every question I asked all she answered was, 'Leave Justin alone.' I looked into her eyes and saw a white hot hate. She would have been happy to cut my throat, but I think she would have been more likely to stab me twenty-one times and claim it was an accident. I happen to be an expert on women like that. She is too much for you, Justin. You are the weak one. She deserves better than you.

"The good news for you is that we are done here. You and Ms. Gordon are free to go. I will have someone drive you back to your apartment. You should be able to suck back a few beers before passing out watching tonight's game."

I watched the Director walk to the door. When she had just pulled the door open I said, "Did you even love them?" It was a mean and rotten thing to say, but her superior attitude just pissed me off. I was tired of playing mouse for this cat.

She turned around slowly. "What did you say?"

"You heard me, April Anne"

She walked over to the table. "Oh, are you trying to grow a backbone, dear? It is too late. It is just not you." Then she leaned over so her eyes were inches from mine. "By the time this is over you will come and beg for my help and give me everything I want." Then she placed her finger on my nose and gave it a push. She walked out of the room without another word.

When Tif and I got back to our apartment we closed the blinds and turned on some music. We searched the apartment for an hour looking for bugs and video cameras. We did not find any.

"I didn't find anything. How about you?" I asked Tif.

"I didn't find anything either. Do you really think she is going to keep us under surveillance?"

"I think she is capable of anything, but Dr. L. was probably right. We are probably not under active surveillance. What happened with you down at OPIE?"

"After they split us up they put me in a little room without windows."

"Me, too. I didn't see how, but I'm sure I was under surveillance."

"I assumed that. No one came for awhile so I just folded my arms on the table, put my head down, and tried to get some sleep. I think she slammed the door to wake me. I was still partly asleep when she sat down. Before she could say anything I told her, 'You are not unattractive for an older woman.' She didn't even flinch. Her response was, 'And you are not unattractive for a younger woman.' Then she proceeded to critique my appearance and offer beauty tips. When she finished she said, 'Of course, you regard all these things as trivial. You regard only inner beauty of importance, but when you are my age people will say that it is too bad, she used to be pretty.'

"Then she pulled out her computer and showed me some surveillance photos from that night when you were so sick. She demanded that I tell her how to find Dr. L. and the underground medical facility. I just told her to leave you alone. She threatened to put me in jail. She threatened to put you in jail. She told me I would lose my job and never be able to work again. She threatened the same thing for you. I just kept repeating the same thing: leave Justin alone.

"We ended up standing up, our faces inches from each other, screaming at the top our lungs. Suddenly she just turned and walked out of the room. When she left I collapsed in the chair exhausted."

"Wow! When she threatened to put you in jail I caved. I told her everything I knew which is precious little."

Tif grabbed me, actually shook me. "You can't do that, Justin. Never give in, that is what they always expect."

"I'm sorry, Tif. I just couldn't take a chance with you. This is not your fight. This is between me and the Director."

"No, Justin, you're wrong. This has never been just between you and the Director. You'll never be alone. She just wants you to feel that way."

"I don't know, Tif. Maybe it's just not worth it. I'm beginning to think more of Dr. L's suggestion. If we move away from here we'll be out of her jurisdiction. Maybe we can put this behind us."

"No, I'll never leave. That would be giving in. Now, shall we have Thai or pizza?"

# Part Four

Tif and I married. It was not as simple as that although Tif is so direct it sometimes feels that way.

For months after being taken down to OPIE we searched for evidence of surveillance. I had spent most of the last year scanning crowds for familiar faces, looking for security cameras, and circling blocks to see if anyone was following, but this was all new to Tif. Neither of us ever found any evidence that we were under surveillance. We decided to follow Dr. L's advice to let the banality of our existence be our shield.

We were never given a bill for the care I received at the underground facility. Dr. L. implied that there was no charge, but Tif and I put together a few thousand in cash for a donation. Maybe we were not expected to pay, but we felt we should.

To take a break Tif and I decided to take a long weekend. We drove to Colorado and climbed up a fourteen thousand foot mountain. On top with the wind blowing and the clouds so close you felt you could touch them I told Tif that I'd like to go higher. She started talking about climbing Mt. Kilimanjaro. "You don't understand," I said. "I want to get married." She sat there with a dumb expression on her face, didn't say anything. "To you," I added.

Luckily I was sitting on the ground. Tif threw herself at me and knocked me over. There was nothing unusual in that. She always knocks me over.

We decided to get married right away. It was a small affair, just family and a few friends. There was something else Tif wanted to do right away, start a family. I found it hard to imagine this wild woman, this force of nature as a mother, but I was in for the ride. We were lucky. Tif got pregnant right away when so many of her friends were still trying after years.

Tif glowed during pregnancy. She is a naturally happy and positive person. Being pregnant turned her up a couple of notches at least until we had less than two months to delivery.

When we started this odyssey the first thing I thought of was healthcare. It turns out there is a whole system of midwives for home delivery. Evidently the women's lobby had kept this area of private care open. I did not know much about midwives. I always thought they were supposed to be a low tech alternative, but Kathy, our midwife, performed a series of ultrasounds. The one she performed with less than eight weeks to go bothered her. She asked us to come back in a few days when she would have a consultant with her. Kathy told us that it was just a precaution.

When we went back the consultant turned out to be a man in his seventies. Kathy introduced him as Paul. He performed the ultrasound this time with Kathy watching. He spent a longer time with the ultrasound than our midwife. After he finished he told us, "I'm going to review the findings with Kathy. She'll be back in a few minutes to discuss them with you."

Neither of us said anything while we waited for Kathy. We were too busy praying. Kathy came back in the longest five minutes of my life. "Tiffany, Justin," she said, "I think the ultrasound shows a cardiac abnormality. That's why I had Paul here today. He's an expert technician with the ultrasound."

"What does this mean?" Tif asked her.

"Maybe nothing, if the abnormality is small enough the baby may not even need surgery."

"What usually happens?"

"The baby may be acutely ill shortly after delivery and need emergency surgery. This type of abnormality is extremely rare. I've never seen one before. The good thing is that this abnormality is not associated with any other abnormalities such as mental retardation so the prognosis is good."

Kathy stopped and waited. We were in shock. Everything had been going so well. We had been running headlong into the adventure of life until this tripped us.

"I know this is a lot to comprehend all at once," Kathy said. "You don't have to make up your mind right now. I'm going to write down the name of the problem so you can look it up on your computers. The information on the computer will give you a more comprehensive view of the problem than I can. I am not an expert in pediatric cardiology. You might want to talk with one. Once you have done that we can talk further, but if you decide to continue with home delivery I will have to ask you to sign a release saying you understand the risks and releasing me from all responsibility."

Kathy made a few more apologies and promised not to abandon us, but it was clear she wanted nothing to do with the delivery.

Out in the car I gave Tif a hug and a kiss. "What do we do now?" I asked her.

"We check this out on the computer and then we make some calls to see if there are any options."

"What about Dr. L.?"

"That's one of the calls I was going to make, but it has been a year since we saw him. Maybe he isn't even alive."

Paul was just leaving the office. "I want to talk with Paul. Are you going to be all right if I leave you alone for a while?"

"I'll go with you."

"No, I think this will go better if there is an audience of one. You stay here."

I caught Paul just as he reached his car. "Paul, could I speak with you a moment?"

Paul raised his hands as if he were expecting an attack. "Look, buddy, it is not my fault. I just read the ultrasounds."

"I'm not angry. I just want information. My wife and have some decisions to make. I thought you might be able to help."

Paul scanned the parking lot. His head swiveled back and forth as if he was expecting someone was trying to sneak up on him. I don't know what he expected to find, but I was familiar with the drill. When he was satisfied that no one was watching he said, "Walk with me."

I let him lead the way. We went the length of one block and turned the corner with him looking over his shoulder every few steps. Half way through the second block he stopped. "Okay. What do you want to know?"

"First, who are you? I always thought midwives were women taking care of women with low tech home deliveries, but our midwife is doing ultrasounds and then you show up."

"Let me tell you about me first. I was an obstetrician. I'm not supposed to mention that so you've never heard it. I can't even mention my medical degree. I retired six years ago from one of the clinics in town. I just got tired of the grind. I had always worked with some of the midwives. The other obstetricians gave me a hard time about that, but I thought that if my advice could save one complication it was the right thing to do. After I retired some of the midwives still called me up asking my opinion. I didn't see any harm in it as I was just discussing the findings of the midwives. I wasn't seeing or treating any patients. Then some of the midwives asked me to consult on ultrasounds which were a specialty of mine before I retired."

"Yeah, what's up with the ultrasounds? I thought midwives were supposed to be low tech."

"When the lay midwife movement started they were no-tech, but midwives decided they needed more drugs and more equipment to better serve their clientele. Lately the rage has been to buy these ultrasounds, although some midwives still go the no-tech route. Now whenever one of the midwives I work with finds something with the ultrasound they call me in to confirm. I didn't think there was any problem with that until I received a visit from OPIE. Do you know what OPIE is?"

"Yeah, unfortunately I do."

"Anyway, a whole bunch of these OPIE agents show up at my house with a search warrant and proceed to toss my house. They were looking for patient records so they even took my computers. One of those little wimps told me I couldn't hang my medical school diploma on the wall of my study because I didn't have a license any more. I even had a visit with the dragon queen."

"The dragon queen?"

"You know, Dr. Stricker, the director of that group of idiots. They came back a couple of months later and tossed my house again. After they had been at it for an hour in walks Dr. Stricker. She glides in like a beauty queen and you think, 'Finally, someone who is not an idiot.'

Turns out she's got a mouth on her like a sailor. She laid down the law. She was going to let me continue as long as no patient ever found out I was a doctor. I think she thought what I was doing was about making money. I was just trying to help people by giving a little advice. I'd go to hell before I let her stop me."

"Unfortunately I know all about OPIE and the Director. What about the results of the ultrasound? What do you think we should do?"

"Well, these new ultrasounds are so cool. Even ten years ago we would not have been able to make a diagnosis. I'm really surprised Kathy was able to make that diagnosis. Believe me, you're lucky that Kathy had access to one of these new ultrasounds and she paid attention in the ultrasound course otherwise you would have delivered at home and been lucky to get the baby to the hospital."

"So, you think we should deliver in a hospital?"

Paul started looking around. "We've been standing here too long. People are starting to notice. Let's walk over to the park. I know a bench that is out of video range."

I followed Paul into the park until he indicated a bench. Before he sat down he did a 360 scan. "Are you always this paranoid?" I asked him.

"It's not paranoia if you know someone has you under surveillance. I wasn't always like this, but ever since my run-ins with OPIE I've tried to be careful. I know they have the midwives I work with under surveillance. I am pretty sure my home is under surveillance. I don't want to give OPIE anything to work with. Now what were you saying?"

"You wouldn't deliver outside the hospital."

"No way! Didn't Kathy tell you that?"

"She said that she didn't want to abandon us, but the message was clear. What would you advise if you can't use the hospital?"

"You're one of those?"

"Yeah, I'm afraid so."

"I always thought you people were a bunch of loonies until I started advising midwives like Kathy. All the couples I've met who can't use the system seem so normal. Unfortunately, if you can't use the system you and your wife are totally screwed."

"Can't we just go to the hospital when she's in labor? Don't they have to take care of her and the baby?"

"Forty years ago that's pretty much what would have happened. You'd end up with a huge bill, but everybody would have been taken care of. Now, everything has changed. First, Kathy cannot deliver your baby.

If someone found out about the ultrasound Kathy would be in big trouble for trying to deliver the baby outside of the hospital. So, that's out. Second, if you go to the hospital for delivery all hell may break loose."

"What do you mean it may break loose?"

"It all depends on who is in charge of your case at the hospital. I've seen similar problems just swept under the rug. If you end up with a red queen you and your wife will end up in jail and you may lose your child."

"Wait. What do you mean by red queen?"

"You must remember 'Alice in Wonderland' where the red queen orders, 'Off with their heads'?"

"Sure."

"Well, there are a lot of red queens running things now and I don't mean just women. And you're middle class. They'll love throwing the book at you."

"I don't get it. How can they do all this stuff?"

"It was a case like yours that convinced me to retire. I had reached retirement age, but I wanted to continue practicing for four or five years more. I had a husband and wife come into the hospital in labor. They were a nice couple of kids, but they had screwed up by not getting the prescribed pre-natal care and they had eligibility issues. It was her first delivery so the labor took a long time. There was some fetal distress so we did a C-section. They decided to watch the baby overnight in the NICU, but that was all it was. The baby did fine. Then I heard that someone was beginning proceedings to take the baby away from this couple. I went to the head of the department involved to find out what the issue was. She told me that all children are really wards of the state and parenting is a privilege that cannot be extended to people who have not been responsible. I thanked her for the explanation, went back to my office, called my superior, and told him I would be retiring."

"I still don't get where the authority comes from to do something like that."

"It's a different psychology. If the government is paying for your healthcare and you equate healthcare with keeping you alive the government owns your life. It's too bad. We were founded on the idea that the government derived its legitimacy from the people as individuals. Now most of us are just the masses waiting for government crumbs and we find out the government needs protection from us.

"I don't know. Perhaps society is just too complicated and the world too populous. Maybe we have to give up individual freedom to live in today's world. It would have been a debate worth having, but the people who wanted this change never wanted an open debate. They would tout the benefits and hide the problems.

"It didn't have to work out this way, at least in healthcare. When the whole healthcare reform thing started I had the idea that if we went to a system of capitation for all services you could control costs. Doctors would be empowered to do exactly what they have always claimed to do act in the best interests of their patients. Management types could help doctors find more efficient ways of delivering care. It would have gotten the government out of the business of restricting care and making life and death decisions into a business they actually had a decent track record at, ensuring quality. There would be a better chance of innovation and the government could actually push the envelope in care instead of boxing it in. The key would be allowing these enterprises to make money. That was always a nonstarter, but the real reason that such a system could never exist was control. The politicians viewed healthcare as a $2.5 trillion slush fund they could use to reward their friends and punish their enemies and, in the name of cost control, they now control you."

Paul just stopped. I waited for him to go on. "I'm sorry. I've been rambling. All those years talking to people everyday, you miss it in retirement. You spend almost fifty years of your life becoming and being a doctor. Then you see what has happened and you become bitter. I guess at least I did. Most people just want healthcare when they want it. They have no idea of the inner workings and no idea what they've given up.

"Now, as to your problem I suggest Canada."

"Canada?"

"Yes. You and your wife go to Canada. When she goes into labor go to one of their major teaching hospitals. If she's far enough along in labor they won't consider transferring her. If your baby is acutely ill they will take care of the problem. The surgery is not new and they will do a good job. You and your wife will have to lie about the ultrasound and they will know you are lying, but if you max out your credit cards to pay them they actually won't mind. It is always nice to have a paying customer. You might want to pay off your credit cards and apply for a new one."

"I can't believe what you're suggesting."

"It's better than spending the next ten years of your life fighting the government for custody of your child. Look, I've been talking too long. I know your wife is waiting for you. You head directly back. I'm going to find someplace to have a cup of coffee. If we show up together that might alert OPIE."

"Is there an OB we should go to if we can work things out here?"

"Ask Kathy who she refers to. I'm sure she has someone you can trust, but no doc is going to be able to help you with this administrative stuff. We're second class citizens in the healthcare world, just well paid technicians."

We stood up and shook hands. "Paul, I want to thank you for spending the time talking with me. It's been a big help."

"No problem, I like to talk."

"One last thing, do you even get paid for advising the midwives?"

Paul gave a short laugh. "Do cookies count?"

We said our farewells. On the walk back to the car I thought about how best to break it to Tif.

When I got in the car the first thing I said was, "Are you okay?"

"I'm fine. You were gone along time. What did he say?"

"He said that we were screwed."

On the way home I laid it all out for Tif. She didn't cry. I could see her getting angrier and angrier. I could see her thinking: try to take my child, someone will pay.

When we got home I went into the nursery. It had been such a pleasure watching Tif decorate this room. A few days ago Tif and I were excited with the possibilities of life. Now I did not even know whether this room would be used. I left and shut the door.

The next couple of weeks we talked about the problem endlessly. We could not make any decisions. Tif talked to some friends who were lawyers. I liked the Canada idea so I applied for another credit card even though I knew Tif hated the idea. Tif contacted Dr. L. who was still alive. He knew of no underground facility that was capable of performing heart surgery on an infant.

The worst part was watching Tif change. Before all this happened she had been excited. She would smile through any problem pregnancy had to offer. Now she never smiled. She seemed angry all the time. She even snapped at me. I knew she was being eaten up from the inside. We both were.

One night we were lying in bed. I couldn't sleep with everything running through my head. I didn't think Tif was asleep either. I squeezed her hand. "What is it?" she said.

"You know I love you?"

Tif rolled over, not an easy job when you are eight months pregnant. "Yes, I know you love me."

"Do you know that I will love you no matter how this turns out?"

"Yes, I know you will love me no matter what."

"Will you love me no matter how this turns out?"

Her answer was a simple, "Yes"

"Then let's get some sleep."

The next morning I walked into OPIE headquarters and asked to see the Director. "Do you have an appointment?" the receptionist asked.

"No," I told her, "just say that Justin Lodge would like to see her."

"Okay, but you'll have to wait."

I found a chair and sat down. I had brought a candy bar, a bottle of water, and some reading material because I was sure I would have to wait.

Two hours later Joey shows up. "Justin, what are you doing here?"

"I came to see the Director."

"I hope this is something good. I was having a good day until someone told me you were here."

"Joey, after this she may positively purr."

Joey ushered me into the Director's office. She was sitting behind the same big desk. Without saying a word or looking up she pointed to one of the chairs on my side of the desk. She was wearing another conservative suit, but the blouse was cut low and she wore a large necklace that hung below the cleavage of the blouse. Her hair and makeup were perfect. I had to wonder what there was about her that made me, who was usually oblivious to such things, notice them and, yes, approve.

"Mr. Lodge, excuse me for not getting up to greet you. I am very busy today, but I tried to make time for an old friend. How is that midwife thing working out for you and Tiffany?"

I wasn't surprised that she knew that Tiffany was seeing a midwife. She was too thorough not to know. There would be time to answer that question later. "I came to apologize."

"Why, Mr. Lodge, whatever for?"

"You know what for. What I said was mean. I was under stress. I didn't really mean it."

"Yes, it was mean of you, but I understand the heat of battle so I hold only a small grudge. Now, what is it that brings you here after all this time?"

I told her all about the ultrasound results and what we were told might happen if Tiffany delivered in a hospital.

"You were correctly informed. I can almost guarantee that it will happen and, despite what you might think, I will not be involved at all. If I were you I would be thinking: Canada, although, India is a possibility. The Indians can be very reasonable where cash is concerned. Unfortunately, this sort of thing is not available on one of those medical cruises out of the Bahamas. That would have been so perfect. You could finish off a few beers and work on your tan while Tiffany was giving birth."

"I don't think Tiffany will do any of those things. She wants to fight."

"Good for her, it is what I would expect. She will lose."

"I thought you liked Tiffany."

"I understand and respect her. That is a little different than like."

"I am begging you to help us."

"I am willing to help you, but you know my conditions."

There it was, the real reason I came here. The rest had been foreplay. "Okay, I will do it, but you have to promise me nothing bad will happen to Dr. L."

"Nothing bad will happen. No one wants someone his age incarcerated. Anyway, most of the inmates would probably consider him a hero. We will just plea bargain him as fast as possible and chip him."

"Chip him?"

"Implant a tracking chip on his body some place he cannot remove it and let him go. It will be good for him. He can finally give up this game he plays and visit his grandchildren."

"Good. Then this is what I propose. I will contact Dr. L. the same way I did last time. He knows of the problem we are having so hopefully he will be willing to set up a meeting without Tiffany. If you give me a single use cell I will contact you with the time and place. I will wear a device you can track. The rest will be up to you. If he outsmarts you again that will not be my fault and you will deliver your part of the deal."

"All right, Justin, we have a deal, but if I find out that you have double crossed me I would advise moving to Canada permanently. Furthermore, I will not deliver my side of the bargain until after the meeting so you don't have much time. Wait outside and Joseph will bring you what you need."

The Director returned to working on her computer. I had been dismissed. I left without saying a good-bye or thank you. Outside I leaned against a wall until Joey showed up. He gave me a cell and a GPS watch. "What did you do? I've never seen her in this good a mood."

I told him, "She won, Joey. She won."

The next day I went around town putting up signs. The signs said, "Dr. L., I need to speak with you in person about our problem. Please contact me at work. Justin." I had a better idea how to contact him so I only put up twenty posters. At the community center where I think I ran into Rodney I even went to the desk and asked the person on duty if it was all right to put up my sign. She read my sign and looked at me. She did not ask any questions such as, "Who is Dr. L.?" What she did say is, "Go ahead. It's a free country."

I did not know what to expect. Would Dr. L. contact me right away? Would Dr. L. contact me at all? I could only hope. With Tif well into her last month I was running out of time.

I came back from lunch on the eighth day after I put up the signs and found an envelope. Inside was a note saying, "Tonight, 8:30, 174 3rd Street, stand on the curb under the street light." I waited for an hour before taking a break. I dialed the preset number and repeated the information on the note. I broke off the communication in seconds. I looked at the hand held computer as if it was broken and pulled out another to call Tif. I had to make some excuse for being out late. Tif did not like it. She was nervous enough without this break in routine. I assured her I was just a call away.

At 8:30 I was standing under a street light. It was a run down section of town with some empty buildings and not too far from the river. I did not see any sign of OPIE. I had to hope the Director was ready. I waited nearly half an hour. He appeared out of the shadows across the street. He was wearing a hat with the collar of his coat turned up. He was the right height, but I could not be sure it was him.

Before crossing the street he waved. I waved back. Not knowing what was expected I stayed glued to my spot. Dr. L. was halfway across the street when I heard the voice of the Director from behind me. "Donald, so nice to see you again."

Dr. L. stopped in the middle of the road. There was the roar of an engine and a white van pulled up between Dr. L. and me. When the van moved on Dr. L. was gone. Two black government sedans moved in to block the van. A figure I thought was Dr. L. ran from the van into an abandoned building.

I turned and started to yell at the Director. "Did you have to…." I stopped in midsentence. I almost didn't believe what I saw. The Director was wearing an OPIE baseball cap, OPIE windbreaker, pants, and sneakers.

"Did I have to what?"

"Did you have to jump out and scare him off that way?"

"Don't worry. He can't get away. I had two shooters mark his coat with homing devices. Before I said anything both shooters reported him tagged. We can follow him wherever he goes. Wait. Here is a report. I'll put it on speaker."

"Director?"

"Here. Go ahead."

"The target appears to be in the northwest corner of the basement."

"Cover all the exits. When all the exits are covered send in a team to retrieve him."

"Director, are we permitted to use force?"

The Director smiled at me before answering. "No, that's a negative to use of force. The target is not armed. There will be no use of lethal force."

The Director started off toward the abandoned building. I didn't move. She turned back. "Did you really expect to hide in the shadows?" she said.

"No, I'm not going," I told her. "You don't need me to capture Dr. L."

"If you expect me to fulfill my side of the bargain you are going to be there right until the end. Donald is going to know who sold him out and you are going to face him knowing that you betrayed his trust. If you try to weasel out now I promise you I will make your life hell."

The Director marched off to the abandoned building. After a second's hesitation I ran to catch up.

The inside of the building was dark. Flashlights were the only source of illumination and they seemed to be everywhere.

A flashlight approached. "Director?"

"Yes, what is it?"

"We found this in the northwest corner of the basement." In the light of the flash it looked like the coat Dr. L. was wearing.

"Oh, you idiots," I said, "he's outsmarted you again."

"No, he hasn't," the Director said. "He can't get out of the building. I want a complete search of the building even if you have to tear down walls and ceilings. Bring in some generators and floodlights."

"We've already started, Director."

The flashlight left us alone. We stood in silence the only light the Director's flash hanging at her side. "Is that what this is all about?" I said. "He's always outsmarted you, hasn't he?"

She shone the flash at my face holding it inches from my eyes. "No, this time we'll get him. We've got the whole area covered by drones. Nothing can move without my knowing about it. You'll see."

Her cell went off. "Yes?"

"Director, come to the second floor. We've found something you need to see."

"I'll be right there." Her flash searched for the stairway. "Over there. You go first."

The stairs shook as we climbed. At the top of the stairs another flashlight greeted us. "This way, Director. The back of the building has a broken window. When someone checked it they found a rope ladder. There are already agents in position on that side of the building. Either he got down the ladder before we got in position or he's still inside."

"Continue on with the search of the building. This may be a ruse to make us think he got away. I'm going down the ladder. I'll take the boy here with me." The Director motioned to me. "You first, Justin."

I wasn't too thrilled at going down the rope ladder. I had seen Dr. L. do it at the hotel but this was twice as far. I crawled through the window feet first and climbed down with the ladder banging the side of the building all the way. The Director was right after me.

When we made it down an agent ran up. "Director, we found a loose manhole cover over there. There were some marks that aren't rusted suggesting it has been moved recently."

The Director just said, "Show me," and we were off again.

The manhole wasn't far away. The cover wasn't close to being in the right position. "Get the cover off there and let's see what's inside."

"There seem to be foot prints, Director."

"Can we get a drone in there?"

"No, we'll lose the signal. Do you want me to go?"

"No, give the boy here your flashlight. He and I will follow the target through the sewers. What are you waiting for, Justin? Climb in."

Two of the agents lowered me into the manhole. The Director followed. There were just two directions to go. The Director noted some splash marks on side walls of the sewer. "It looks like he headed north. We'll follow the sewer line and see if we can head him off." The Director turned to me, "Get crawling, boy. Now you're going to see what life is really like."

I started crawling through the muck with the Director close behind. I hadn't been crawling long before the Director started in on me. "How do you like it now, boy? You're lucky it hasn't rained today. The water level might be up to your neck." She started prodding me with her flashlight. "Get moving, boy. We'll never catch him at this rate. Do you think any of this would bother Dr. Love? Get crawling, boy." And she went on and on. Strangely, it motivated me to crawl faster, anything to shut her up.

At the next manhole I just kept right on going. At the one after that there was a branch to the right. I thought I saw a light. I decided to go down that branch without asking permission, anything to keep ahead of her and out of range of her flashlight. The Director followed.

"Why did you turn down here?" the Director asked.

"The water seemed muddier and I thought I saw a light."

"The boy takes some initiatives. I am so surprised."

And I was surprised when she shut up, but I still kept crawling as fast as I could.

We passed through several more manholes. Eventually we connected with a culvert that was big enough to walk through. The culvert emptied out into the river. I got out into the water, waited for the Director, and helped her to shore. She had her hand held computer out as soon as she hit dry land.

"We just came out of a culvert at the river just south of the bridge. We haven't spotted the target. Does the command center have any video on the target?"

"We don't have any drones working the area, Director."

"Doesn't somebody have eyes on the target?"

I did. Someone was climbing toward the bridge. "There he is."

"The target is climbing toward the bridge. Have someone close off the other side. Close in on this side but do not approach the target. I'm climbing to the bridge now."

The Director led the way up the river bank to the bridge. When we arrived there were two cars blocking this side of the bridge. There were two more cars on the far side of the bridge. In between, caught in the headlights, was the target, Dr. L. He seemed confused. His head swiveled this way and that as if he was searching for a way out.

The Director walked a few steps onto the bridge. I was just a step behind her. She turned and pointed to two agents. "Hold the boy. Whatever happens don't let him go."

The two agents grabbed my arms. I tried to shake them off, but not very hard. I didn't know why she ordered them to hold me.

The Director took a few more steps onto the bridge. "Donald," she yelled, "it's time to stop. Give up so we can all go home."

Dr. L did not say anything. He took off his coat, took off his shoes, and started to climb the railing.

I did not realize what was about to happen until Dr. L. was standing on the railing. When I did I stomped on the foot of the agent holding my right arm. He let go of my right arm which I used to hit the agent holding my left arm in the jaw. He loosened his grip and I shook free. Then I ran past the Director. I was almost to Dr. L. when a voice in front of me yelled, "Stop."

I stopped. I was only ten feet away from Dr. L. He was standing on the railing facing me, one hand holding onto an upright, the other held up to say, 'Stop.' He smiled. He held his arms out from his side at shoulder level, looked up to the sky, and fell over backwards.

I had gotten my shoes and jacket off and was climbing the railing when they reached me. The two agents dragged me down forcing me to my knees. Other agents were scanning the river with their flashlights. The Director strolled up. She was back, the beauty queen, regal despite being covered with filth.

One of the agents holding me asked, "What should we do with him, Director?"

She stood over me. "Let him go."

"But he assaulted a Federal agent?"

"Yes, he did. I am sure the inability of two agents to hold onto a wimp like this will look good on your fitness report, but by all means include the assault in your report. Perhaps we will find an opportunity to file charges at a later date."

The two agents let me go. I could not find the energy to stand up. The Director walked over to the railing and looked over the side. She turned to face me. "Like it down in the dirt?" she asked. I didn't answer.

"You know," she said, "at one time the price was thirty pieces of silver. Now I guess it is just healthcare."

The Director glided away. I pulled myself to my feet and stepped to the railing. I looked down to see spotlights searching the dark waters. My only thought was: What have I done?

# Epilogue

I went home and lied to my wife. I am not proud of that. In fact I despised myself for it. I despised myself for everything about this affair. I thought Tif and I and our unborn daughter had been unfairly caught in this battle between Dr.L. and the Director. I was just trying to get out from between them. I was just trying to get our healthcare back so we could go on as a family. I guess it was wrong of me to expect someone else to pay the price. How was I to know that his freedom was a price he would not pay? Everything had turned out horribly, horribly wrong.

The Director was true to her word. The next day a messenger delivered a package to me at work. The package contained personal health records in the names of Justin I. Lodge and Tiffany Gordon Lodge. There was a letter apologizing for the unfortunate computer glitch that had caused the problem. The letter explained the use of the personal health records and referenced a toll free number to use if there were any problems. There was even a personal note from the Director.

As soon as I got home from work I showed Tif the personal health records and letter from OPIE. It took only a second for her to ask, "What did you do?"

I had been dreading this moment. Any way I put it I had given in and I was married to the 'Never Give In' girl. Worse, did Tif already know the story?

"I went and begged the Director," I told her.

"I find it hard to believe that woman would give any advantage away," she said.

"No, no, you've got to remember that the Director was a wife and mother who lost her family in a tragic car accident. She feels for you." I can't believe I was apologizing for the Director. "Besides, she likes you. Here is what she wrote: Dear Mr. Lodge, You have my fondest hope for the safety of your wife and unborn baby girl. Hopefully, she will turn out like her mother. We can always use more strong women. Warmest regards, April Anne Love Stricker."

Tif did not challenge me anymore on this issue. She was too busy trying to set up an appointment with an OB for the next day.

My plan was to confess everything to Tif sometime in the future, sometime after she had delivered, sometime after our child had recovered from surgery, sometime when we had returned to normalcy and the sun was shining.

I still had a little hope. They never found Dr. .L's body. I searched the computer everyday to see if a body was reported any where down river. Also, I searched for any mention of the death or funeral arrangements for Dr. Donald Love. After five days a body was reported a hundred miles downstream. I thought that was it. The next day it was identified as a fisherman who had disappeared the week before.

I waited over a week and called Joey. "I'm not supposed to be talking to you," he said.

"Joey, you owe me. All I want to know is whether the body of Dr. Donald Love was ever recovered. Please, I've got to know."

Joey said, "I'll see what I can do." He broke the connection.

Joey called back the next day to tell me that the body had never been found, but the case file was closed.

Joey's call gave me hope. I tried to convince myself that Dr. L. was still alive. Everything he had done that night had been sloppy. Dr. L. was not sloppy. Surely he could have hidden from us in one of the buildings or in the sewers. It was like he was leaving us a trail to follow, leading us to the bridge so he could fake his own death. I even entertained the idea that it was not Dr. L. at all, but one of his many friends. I knew better. I had seen him from less than ten feet away. I was convinced at that moment it was Dr. L. on the railing. I know I had seen Dr. L. go over. I had seen him letting go.

I was not sleeping well. Tif thought I was just anxious about the baby. That played a role, but the real problem was that I would wake up in the middle of the night and play over and over the seconds when Dr. L. held out his arms, looked to the sky, and fell over backwards. That was not as bad as the time I dreamed I was Dr. L. falling, falling until I woke up with a start.

Tif went into labor a week after her due date. The labor took a long time. We named our child Ruth. Once Ruth was delivered everything moved much faster. Ruth went directly into the NICU. In less than 48 hours she was in surgery. Almost two weeks passed before we could hold her and over two weeks before we could take her home.

The time in the hospital had been a respite from my visions of Dr. L. falling off the bridge. With Ruth at home the visions and dreams returned. I started chasing down any person of the appropriate height who was wearing a hat and who had a collar turned up so his face could not be seen. I do not think I expected to find him, but I had to look. My search was crazy, but it was the only thing keeping me from going flat out insane.

About three months after Ruth was born I was approached by a male in his forties. I recognized him immediately as the man who followed me from the community center. He slapped an envelope against my chest. "This is from Dr. L." He walked off.

I took a moment before I understood what he said. If this was a letter from Dr. L. then Dr. L. was alive. I ran after him. When I caught him I asked, "Does this mean that Dr. L. is alive?"

He grabbed the front of my jacket and pulled back one hand as if he was going to hit me. "Alive? You ask me whether he's alive, you, the one that killed him."

He pulled back his arm farther. I prepared to receive a blow. The blow never came. He just collapsed in tears. "You're Rodney, aren't you?"

"Yes. Dr. L. was my best friend."

"If he's dead when did he give you this letter?"

"The day he died he gave it to me and asked me to deliver it if anything happened. I didn't want to deliver it. I didn't think you deserved it, but I decided I owed it to Dr. L."

"I don't understand. Are you saying Dr. L. expected to die?"

"We all told him not to go, but he just wanted so much to help you. He felt responsible for what was happening to you. I think he thought he would go and meet with you and if it turned out to be a trap he would just let himself be captured. When the time came he couldn't do it. He couldn't give in."

"You don't know how sorry I am. Ever since it happened I've been looking for someone to say that to."

Rodney just said good-bye and left. I looked at the envelope. It had my name on it. I decided to wait until later to read it.

At 2::00 a.m. Ruth was crying. I walked her until she fell asleep. Rather than put her back in her crib I sat in the rocking chair and read the letter. It was written, not printed from a computer. I do not think I have ever received more than just a short note in handwritten form. Here is what it said:

Dear Justin,

If you are reading this letter then I am dead. I am writing this because I know you will blame your self. You will not be able to let it go, but you must let it go or the blame will destroy you. What happened was my choice.

It is my hope that you and Tiffany and your child can know peace now. If I had not desired to tell my story this would never have happened to you. I know now that it was the last vestiges of egotism, the sin of pride, to think there is anything remarkable about your self, anything worth telling. It would be wrong to let you pay the price of my sin.

It is my hope that the Director will be free to become April Anne again. Her obsession with me was totally beyond any reason considering how little I did. I represented something to her that neither of us can explain. Perhaps the fact that I knew her so many years ago turned my acts into a personal crime against her. Perhaps her obsession will find another object. I hope not. My wish for her is to be free.

You remind me of my self. Rodney would tell you I say that about everybody. I do. It is my way of saying I see the human in all of us while celebrating the particular. In your case the comparison is more acute. I once was a young man with a family. I gave up on my values to do what I thought was best for my family. Many years later when I realized what I had done I wondered if it might have been different if I had spoken out, if I had lived my own values. It would not have taken much to steer a different course. So, I sought redemption. I spent much of the last few years living on the streets, hiding from the Director and OPIE.

This always upset my many friends, but I could not put them at risk, I could not explain to them that the only thing that mattered was helping people that needed my help. I never thought of it as a hard life. It was just life and I loved every minute of it.

You will not have the luxury of time. Your crisis is upon you as I write. If I am dead you will seek redemption because you will not be able to give up your personal responsibility. You will seek redemption so that you can look in your wife's eyes and not wonder what she sees in you.

Let me give you a little advice in your quest for salvation. Do not try to save the world, save yourself, and in saving yourself the world will be saved. Remember the words of my first underground patient. Freedom means having choices. You have choices, but you have to take your life into your hands.

Your friend,

Donald Love

I put Ruth into her crib, sat down, and read the letter again. He was right, of course. I loved Tif, but I wondered what she would think when I told her the truth. How could I ever be worthy of her respect or even my own?

I thought back to my life before all this happened. I had been drifting, unaware of the reality. In some ways it would be pleasant to go back to that state of innocence. I was not that person any more. I did not want to go back to drifting.

The problem was what could I do? I did not really know very much. My job had taught me some technical matters regarding claims in home and auto insurance. What I did know is what I had experienced regarding the problems surrounding healthcare and underground medicine. The only other thing I had any idea how to do was to write. I resolved to start writing the next day.

I tried sitting down with my computer to write. I remembered that all my computers had been invaded. Maybe I did not want what I was going to write to end up being read by some cyber snoops. I decided to buy a new computer without a net connection.

The next day I went to a computer store and asked for a computer without a connection to the net. The salesperson asked me why I would want that. I told him that I just wanted something simple to keep a journal on and I wanted to keep it private. He told me that they did not carry computers without a connection to the net. I asked if there was someway of disabling it. He told me that was against the law and walked away.

I tried another store. I got basically the same answers, but this time the clerk told me that it was not an actual law, more of a regulation.

I called one of my old roommates, an expert in computers. I got part way through my explanation and he interrupted me saying, "I don't have time right now. Let's meet at our old bar at 6:00."

He was sitting at the bar when I arrived. We had a beer and discussed old times. I started to ask about my problem, but he cut me off. He surveyed the room as casually as possible. "I'm sorry I can't help. Here's some money for the beer.' He got up and left. I paid for the beer. In the bills he had slipped to me was a note with an address and instructions. I was right back in the undercover world.

I went to the address the next day. It turned out to be a hole in the wall computer store. Following instructions I went to the repair counter, dropped the note on the floor, and said, "I'd just like to talk computers."

The owner of the store told me, "If you'd like to use the bathroom it is back there."

I followed his directions and waited in the bathroom. About five minutes later he entered the bathroom, turned on the water, and flushed the toilet. "My understanding is that you want a computer without a net connection. You're not a cyber hobbyist, are you?"

"No, but what is the big deal. All I want to do is some writing and I want to keep it private."

"Well, there's the problem. There is no privacy anymore. All computers double as phones or TV's or movie theatres so they all have net connections. If you have a connection you can be traced. If you don't have a connection it is presumed you are hiding something. Over a decade ago a regulation was written that effectively makes it impossible to buy a computer without a connection. It sounded as if you're getting something for free. No one was going to complain. The big corporations want to invade your privacy even more than the government. For most people it does not matter. There is so much information out there no one can make sense of it all, but do something that interests somebody and you can't get away. I presume you are going to do something that might interest somebody."

"That is a possibility."

"I don't want to know. I can sell you a brand name computer that will have an active connection that will not work. The software that controls the connection will have a virus that disables it. If someone takes an interest in your computer they will be able to track your location, but they won't be able to get inside. If you are ever caught you can always claim you were too stupid to know any better. Will that do?"

"I think so."

"Come back next week at the same time and I will have it ready. This will be a cash transaction."

I now had a secure computer. What was I going to do with it? I had some strange idea of using an old technology, the newspaper. Newspapers had pretty much died as a major force, but I had a friend in college called Terry who brought out an underground paper. At the time I laughed it off and asked him why did he bother? He promised me that someday I would understand. I found him through some mutual friends and asked him out for lunch.

We spent the lunch getting reacquainted, catching up on old classmates. The bill came. I offered to pay. While I was settling up Terry got to the point. "It has been great seeing you again, but I get the feeling there is more to it than old memories. What's an apolitical guy like you want with me?"

"Let's just say I have some experiences that I have converted into software that you might be interested in."

"You're talking in riddles. Is there some reason for your paranoia?"

"That's the problem with paranoia. You can never be sure. In any case it has been great seeing you. I have this baseball cap from our old school. I thought you might like it."

I walked out. In the cap I had secreted a drive with a story about underground medicine. I thought of it as the first in a series that might grow into a book. I didn't know whether it was any good and I didn't know if Terry could use it. The answer came at work about a week later. Terry left a message. "Enjoyed our lunch. I can always use a lunch like that. Call me when you're ready for more." Terry was going to use the piece and wanted more.

I did not relish getting into a slugging match with OPIE. I was not ready. I needed to do a lot more research. Now I had only my personal experiences, but some day I would have more. I had made my choice.

I was feeling better about myself. There was, of course, a more important matter. I waited until a day came that seemed full of my wife's laugh and my daughter's giggles, a day when the sun shone. There was no point in putting it off any longer. I suggested getting some ice cream. We were sitting in the car with our cones when I started my confession. I could not look at her. I had practiced what I would say over and over. There was no right way to tell someone that you have been lying to them and that you betrayed and caused the death of someone you both love. I ended by saying, "I love you, but I'd understand if you want a divorce. Despite what Dr. L. said in his letter I'll never forgive myself. I'll spend the rest of my life making amends."

I do not know what I expected Tif to say. What happened was not on the list. "Give me your ice cream. It's melting." I handed it to her and she shoved it in my face.

"What was that for?"

"For being a big jerk, you big jerk, and not having any faith in me."

She kissed me, ice cream and all. "You asked me whether I would love you no matter how this turned out. I said, 'Yes.' It was all you ever had to know."

So, the 'Never Give In' girl was not giving up on me. I felt better, but there was more to tell. On the drive home I told Tif about the article in the underground paper and my plan to investigate the failings of the healthcare system especially those people who are forced to seek the care they need from underground medicine. I finished by saying, "I've started this, but I can stop. You and Ruth are involved in anything I do. It is our future together. We came very close to a disaster. Just say the word and I will stop."

Tif did not answer right away. She was looking in the back seat where Ruth was sleeping. "It is about Ruth's future," she said. "If we let their control of healthcare control us, stop us from doing what we feel is right what future do we have? I'm in."

"They could take our healthcare away again?"

"I've always wanted to see India. Now let's get Ruth home and to bed. I think it's time we started work on her brother." That was Tif.

A day came when Ruth was almost one year old and Tif wanted to take her on a stroll. She suggested an old estate that had been converted to a park. It was on a hill overlooking the city. There was the mansion kept open as a museum and the gardens. We spent the afternoon strolling through the gardens. It was a good way to spend the day.

The sun was setting. Tif wanted to get on the road before the sun went down. We headed back and loaded Ruth in her seat. The parking lot offered a panoramic view of the sunset. It was so beautiful that I hesitated before getting back in the car. It came to me that this is where Dr. L. had applauded the sunset. Later that night he had met Rodney. In a sense this is where it all began. I looked in at Tif and Ruth and back at the sunset. The moment was so perfect I did not want to leave. I took one more look at the sunset. In the dying light, way off on the brow of the hill I thought I saw a lone figure stand and applaud the glory of the evening.